SPOUSE DISPOSAL

A Novel by

Marvin L. Patton

And

Carol J. Gerrior-Patton

DEDICATION

Carol and I dedicate this book to our parents, siblings, children, and mentors that all played a crucial role in our development and recognition of how different each one saw us and responded to our imaginations; with encouragement, interest, ideas, challenges, and editing, editing, editing.   We have had the honor and privilege to look through the lenses of history, teachers, political figures, writers, and artists, musicians, politicians, church fathers, as well as military figures, businessmen, and our neighbors who had a passion for living, and understanding the reasons for it. Finally, we now have the time to pen our stories down for all who will read them; to entertain, stimulate, educate, as well as laugh and cry if something touches their hearts.

We also dedicate this to Marvin's military family, and Carol's Acadian Gerrior family. Last, but not least, to you the readers. Thank you.

CHAPTERS

ACKNOWLEDGMENTS

Mary Edith Nelson, Virginia Flatter, Michael Hargraves, Almut McCauley, Vernon Patton, John and Ardeth Gerrior, William D. Gerrior, Carmelita DeYoung, Bud Boetticher, Jack Valenti, James A. Michener, and Linda Wilson.

Elsa glared at her tall husky husband with loathing as she shoved the truck's cigarette lighter firmly into its chrome socket. She realized, as she watched him float through the gears of his newly refurbished Freightliner—with strong mighty hands that once impressed her—that she no longer loved her mate of three years. J. Winston Walker, as far as she was concerned, was a man who valued the open road more than he valued her, even when he spent a few days at home, he had a way of making her feel like a worn out piece of furniture instead of his wife; always talking about his experiences and how great it was to have a little *gypsy in his soul—and a strong love for the open road.* She called him Jay, short for James. His close friends sometimes referred to him as *Jay Walker* or *Wind Walker*, due to his trail blazing style—driving in all sorts of weather: hot, cold, windy, braving the elements in all 48 states and Canada; driving up to eight to eleven hours a day.

And now, by finally admitting that she had no more love for her husband, it was time for a change. Especially for the sake of her sanity and physical well-being; she decided it was time to leave, time to get out of the lonely marriage that had brought on deep, crippling periods of depression, and strong bouts of anxiety (panic attacks); making it hard, at times, to breathe and to focus. She felt that every part of her life was out of kilter; almost at a complete stand-still; and the pressing thoughts of having to live in what she called, '*their rundown old house*,' when he left for another road trip was unbearable. For weeks on end he would leave her alone and she detested her life. The wife of a truck driver, from her viewpoint, was far, far too beneath her station—she was waiting on his life, not hers, and it was too lonely for her to continue in such a lifeless and unromantic existence.

Her doctors had given her anti-anxiety pills and a prescription for depression, but so far only the Valium had helped her to overcome the anxiety she felt, and that was far too often. She didn't want to end up becoming a slave to the yellow pills, or any medications for that matter. The changes and side effects of the anti-depressants (she had tried several) had made her feel too lethargic and useless, almost as though she were a zombie. She stopped taking them all together when she felt death closing in; and was shocked to see how she had become a hoarder— keeping every piece of mail, every newspaper, and every magazine, afraid to throw them out, even the letters mistakenly delivered to their address; both personal letters and monthly bills were stacked in boxes, ignored and unread. She had also sought comfort in the arms of other men, which she had soon discovered was not an option for her. She didn't want the guilt and fear of getting caught for cheating. It was a ghastly feeling that made her feel cheap and more wretched. But the loneliness had overpowered her, and for the past two months she had started seeing Jay's ex-boss, Franklin Pierce; a man she realized was much too demanding and demeaning. She tried on several occasions to end the affair but he was holding it over her head. Unknown to her at the time of their affairs, he had secretly recorded their sexual rendezvous. And then, when she tried to end their relationship, he had gleefully shown her and promised—with a wicked grin and an ominous glint in his shadowy eyes—to mail copies of the tapes to her husband, her relatives, and her friends. She felt trapped and betrayed by someone who had, or so she thought, truly cared about her emotions and plight. For her sinful acts she had made her life a living hell; tormented by threats and self-destructive periods of guilt; a neurotic women walking on pins and needles whenever Jay came home, nervously watching for the mailman; turning her cell phone off to avoid Franklin's calls; afraid to go out for an evening dinner date, fearful they might run into the blackmailer.

But tonight, despite the damning videos, she had ended the relationship, telling Franklin he could do whatever he wanted with the tapes. She told him it was over, she was no longer going to be a victim of his blackmailing demands; a slave on his immoral boat that snaked its way through the nights and days of her life, making her feel like a hostage to all his vile and deviant sexual cravings. Elsa was on her way out and she would destroy him if he showed the tapes to anyone, or mailed them to anyone. She also assured him that it would be he, not her, who would eventually pay an ugly price if he released the tapes. 'You talk too much after sex, Franklin' she told him. 'You told me too many things and I have it all on a

11

digital recorder. I know about your new business deals and your political aspirations—release the tapes and everything you are working for will be flushed down the drain. You'll lose everything, Franklin. As for me, I have nothing to lose but my husband. But that's over and you can shove your tapes where the sun doesn't shine. I don't love Jay, nor do I need or want him in my life as of today. Moreover, knowing how Jay can be when betrayed, he'll no doubt come after you and expose you for the sexual depraved degenerate animal that you truly are.'

Elsa waited for the cigarette lighter to pop out as she thought things out. She had made up her mind that she needed happiness and freedom to live her own life on her terms—to do what she needed to do to be content—to climb the social ladder that she had always longed for. She had taken the first step towards her new goal when she made the call. That had been rather easy. But to end her marriage was going to be a little harder to do—as she needed to avoid the courts; she just did not have the money for a good lawyer.

She was a broken vessel in a world of madness and unfulfilled dreams. One after another, there were dead ends, no financial means, no family she could really count on, fading youth, no rudder to steer her boat; no sails to help her maneuver through the known and unknown complications that always, like a swollen river overflowing its banks, drowning all your hopes and dreams with an onslaught of raging chaos and unwanted codswallop. Clearly, in her mind, Jay was at the root of all her heartaches and disappointments. She obviously had picked the wrong man to be with; her heart was dark and in the shadows of hopelessness; her soul was riding on the cold winds of sadness; and she hated those feelings with too much trepidation.

Elsa admitted her marriage to Jay had been a wonderful union at the start, but during the past year she'd become disenchanted with every aspect of their lives and also had become restless and bitter, knowing she would end up doing something that would have expensive consequences. No matter what, she wanted to escape her current situation. She felt victimized and subservient, and there was nothing in the marriage for her to feel reassured about, or truly loved. She wanted and needed more than what her life with Jay had to offer. It was just awful with him, and it flat out didn't matter. She couldn't put a finger on the exact moment she'd lost all feelings for him or when she became so insanely bored by his dullness, or cared how hard he worked to make their lives comfortable, she desired more. Oh, oh, oh, so much more. It was time for a change she thought, a big change. It was time for caviar and oysters instead of hamburgers, hot dogs, tacos, pizzas, or

Chinese take outs. It was time for lovely dinners with champagne and martinis instead of cheap wines, stale beers, or sodas; live theater instead of DVD's or TV. She breathed a sigh so deep in her chest that it burned. Her obvious mood wasn't even getting Jay's attention. As she continued to watch him from the corner of her eyes, she drifted into a dreamlike fantasy of the sort of perfect man she thought she deserved who could provide her with all the things she wanted. A muscular, tanned, six foot two blue eyed blond, with strong powerful arms to hold her, a broad hairy chest to lay her head on--to breathe in the perfumed pheromones of his scent. Oh yes, and a long gorgeous neck she could nibble on. Not to mention he had to be a great ballroom dancer who loved to tango and waltz so carefree over the floors of ballrooms. He'd have to be a brave hunk-of-a-man that was fearless, yet one who possessed sincerity and gentleness with a sweet and quiet disposition, which would always be, without complaint, extremely generous when she wanted something, putting her first, meeting all her womanly needs, no matter what she asked for or desired. She felt a warm sensual bliss shudder through her body just thinking about it and slowly exhaled a hot stream of air from her nostrils. She continued the out of body experience, dreaming about the wonderful man who would be more than honored to go out of his way just to make her happy, no matter the cost, as money would be no object when it came to pleasing her whims. Yes, she needed to find a man who had access to unlimited funds, perhaps from an inheritance or from his line of work? Maybe he could own a tech company in Silicon Valley, she thought. Wealth that would catapult her into a completely higher and elite social strata, completely alien from the life she had to endure with Jay.

A remembrance of Jay's voice interrupted her thoughts. Last night he, for the hundredth time, made a promise: "*I can take care of you, and our children, when we eventually have some. And I won't need any help, no handouts from anyone, no way, I'm tellin ya, J. Winston Walker's family will never take handouts. We'll eat pork and beans and survive on bread 'n water before we take charity.*" Jay would tell her whenever she tried to talk him out of his plans. "*You just wait and see. Within a few more years I'll have three more trucks, hire good reliable drivers that like the road, and have a small trucking company. I can do it. I have accounts and I'm on good terms with National Beef and Tyson Meats. And three produce companies out of Yakima, Selah, and Wenatchee will always have loads of apples, pears, and cherries for me to take back east because the load always come first. It's a win-win situation for everyone. Companies will always need us 'cause I'm never late delivering their products with no losses. Our company will be extremely busy and the money will come in*

17

and within five years we'll have that nice country home with twenty to thirty acres with our own beef and sheep and our own garden. It'll take us a bit of hard work but it'll all work out. It's all planned out and working right now, just the way I laid it all out for you. And within five years, I'll be home to take care of everything. I promise".

I promise, echoed in her ears so many times she thought about screaming at him, to stop telling her anything about his damn dreams of the future. She hated the sound of his voice whenever he explained his plans for the future; she just couldn't bear to hear them again; not one more time. She thought of asking him to take her back home, but she adjusted her seat and again sighed deeply, with an indiscernible moan. Then she glanced at the door, thinking she could survive if she jumped out the next time Jay slowed for a curve, but then changed her mind. "It would be stupid to do that," she said under her breath… She thought: I just need to be patient. This lousy marriage is just that, lousy, and it isn't going to last much longer, that she was sure of.

Elsa hadn't noticed the cigarette lighter had popped out. It was now too cold to light her cigarette; so, she firmly, with a slight attitude, shoved the lighter back in to wait for it to heat back up again. She sucked in a nostril flaring deep breath and slowly turned the gold pinky ring on her little finger next to her wedding ring. She looked down at it and tried again to recall just when and where she had acquired the ring. It had always been there, but that wasn't true. Had Jay bought it for her when they first started dating? No, he wasn't into giving her jewelry. Perhaps her aunt had given it to her when she was in her teens? She just couldn't remember. She'd never taken it off because it was too tight, no matter how hard she tried.

She kept sighing deeply, trying to get Jay's goat, and stopped turning the ring. Nothing ever caught his attention when she wanted it and there was no sense in trying to get the ring off. She had tried and tried far too many times, but the pinky ring was still on her finger. Elsa didn't need the ring to frustrate her any more than what she was already feeling. She went back to thinking about her dream boat, the sort of man she intended to find. One who would take her out of this humdrum existence? A man with plenty of influential connections and filled with lots of daring and strength. The excitement would never cease to amaze her. "I could live with that," she said softly and then smiled as she removed the lighter from its socket.

"Did you say something," Jay asked for the second time.

She ignored Jay as she lit her cigarette. "Not really," she said after exhaling most of the smoke from her first deep draw on her Winston. As she shrugged her shoulders she said casually, "*It's nothing*".

"You sure," Jay asked.

"I'm sure," Elsa said, and then puffed on her cigarette again as she slipped back into thoughts of her extravagant future, losing herself in the wild intoxicating visualizations. She mused that every day would be a day full of surprises. Everyone would find her interesting and desirable; sending her invitations to all the best events and celebrity filled parties that always gave expensive gifts afterwards as tokens of their gratitude that she'd graced them with her beautiful presence and amazing whit; her profound sense of wisdom that was always being circulated through the circles of high society.

Furthermore, Elsa and her new husband would thrill and amaze them all with their beautiful ballroom dancing and her exquisite gowns and jewels. Everyone would try to sway her, insisting that she stay and be part of their inner circle, because she had the ability to bring a refreshing sense of nobility to high society, and all it had to offer. She would be the "IT" girl, living in such a magnificent and expensive world of unlimited extravagances.

She smiled at the thought and then realized how cold it was outside the truck and wondered if it was going to be another freezing, record breaking January night again. Jay had just turned onto the Newport Highway, heading north, leaving Spokane, Washington, behind in a haze of bright lights that illuminated the dark low heavy gray clouds just lurking above the bitter frozen landscape. A good three feet of snow covered the terrain, but for the most part the highway had been plowed and sanded to make traveling through the rugged and awesome Selkirk Mountains less treacherous.

"What did you say," Jay asked for the third time?

"It was nothing. Just thinking," Elsa replied as she continued to look out her window at the trees and snow berms alongside the highway. "It's not worth repeating," she said.

"What's bugging you, Pidge," Jay asked, flicking his headlights on high beam. He wanted this to be a fun outing for them, spending time together.

"You know what's bugging me—and don't call me Pidge. I hate that name," she said, despising Jay's quiet and resolved manner. "And I hate traveling in this weather and in this——this big rig of yours. Especially with that loud and obnoxious refrigerated——"

"It's a reefer." Jay said a bit sharply, cutting his wife off.

"That's what people call weed, you idiot," Elsa said with disgust. "Marijuana. You ever hear of that stuff," she asked tightlipped and smug? Elsa grinned, knowing full well that her words had cut him deeply, perhaps slicing a piece of his heart out. And

23

she knew her night with Jay was just beginning. Tonight's journey through the cold snow-covered and icy road was going to be an enjoyable one, but pure misery for the man she now despised with every inch of her body and soul.

Jay sighed in disbelief, knowing full well his wife knew what he was talking about. Nonetheless, just to have some conversation, he explained it again. "It's a refrigerated unit, runs on diesel at temperature set points, to keep the shippers products safe, either from freezing or from thawing."

"Whatever," Elsa said with a shrug. "It drives me nuts!"

"Since when?" he asked.

"Take a guess." She mocked.

"You still on that kick? Seriously," Jay asked? He knew the gloves were on, with a world class prize fighting ball breaker of a woman; the red-headed all time champion man-eater.

Elsa shrieked so loud she almost choked on her words, "You quit a good job. And for what, driving a damn truck?"

"Don't start on me again. Please!" Jay begged. He hated fighting with her. It was another story for Elsa though, she loved belittling him, every chance she got, she would try to crush him into giving up his job.

"The man who knows it all, Jay Walker," she sneered in a nasally high pitched tone laced with sarcasm that shook the inside of the cab of the truck. "The award winning driver of the year." She laughingly mocked in a wild shrill, shaking her head. "The man with gypsy in his soul. The man who must roll up and down the highways and byways of every godforsaken road from coast to coast and from north to

25

south, to keep the wheels of commerce rolling—to keep America alive and well—to get the freight in on time." Elsa glanced at Jay who was quietly biting his lower lip and gripping the steering wheel, trying to maintain his composure. From her vantage point, Elsa knew she was getting under his skin. She smiled after taking a drag on her cigarette and inhaled deeply into her lungs and then continued her onslaught. "The big man who loves to cross mountains in all kinds of weather; the man who loves to drive across wind-swept prairies, filled with tumbleweeds, and through sand storms, tornadoes, and down crowded and hazy freeways; through Chicago at night, listening to Michael Franks' cool jazz, enjoying the big city lights. Driving through anything to get the loads, light or heavy, to their destinations on time; schedules stated on all those hideous bills of laden. The big man who tells everyone it's the truckers who keep America alive."

"It's true," Jay said firmly. "Besides, this pays more." Jay sighed, doing his utmost to ignore Elsa's sarcasm. "You know that."

"Why didn't you go to work for my dad," she asked with disgust? He needs your———"

"He hates me," Jay interjected firmly.

"That's absurd," Elsa said almost hissing the words out. "Whatever gave you that idea?"

Jay shook his head, knowing full well that he would not have a moment of piece during the ride from Spokane to Sandpoint. "It's not absurd," he said between clinched teeth. "He's done nothing but put me down since the day we met. Besides, if I went to work for him, he'd have his boot up my ass every minute of the day."

"That's ridiculous! You're such a wimp, you're impossible! All Dad ever did was try to make a man out of you," Elsa said coldly.

"Your father hates me. You know it. I know it. So just drop it."

"He doesn't hate you," Elsa said.

"Sure he does. He told me."

"It's your religious beliefs he can't stand." Jay shook his head and sighed deeply. "Every time someone brings up religion," Elsa went on bitterly, "you're right in there with your, _know it all attitude_." She paused to draw on her smoke. "That's what my father, and everyone else we know, dislikes about you, including me."

Jay kept quiet and hoped his wife would get the message and keep still herself. He really had hoped this would have been different for them. But he knew it wouldn't work, as it never did. Elsa, once on a subject, had to attack it from every direction until _she_ was satisfied.

"Look what happened the last time we drove up for a visit," Elsa began after another long draw on her Winston, "Carl brought up abortion rights. You just had to stick your nose into the discussion, bringing up the moral ethics of it, talking about how life begins at conception and that an abortion was an act of murder."

"It is. They just don't want to face up to the truth. The reality of what's done to a fetus is hideous, a cruel form of torture. There's no doubt it feels the pain, the murderous pain, being sucked out of the mother's womb. Some killed with a nail in the side of their heads. I've seen videos. Half, if not all of the women, would change their minds if they would only take the time to truly see it for what it is, indoctrinated murder."

"An abortion is not murder," Elsa said sternly. "An abortion is an abortion. Nothing more."

"There's a documentary about children that starts from conception and goes all the way up to three year olds," Jay went on, ignoring Elsa's calloused statement. "The

29

experts say the scientific research has found that the fetus has a heart, a brain, and a spinal cord in the first few weeks. And it also starts to learn, even at that age."

"Oh shut the hell up," Elsa said venomously. "A woman has the right to do anything she likes with her own body." By this time Elsa felt incensed. She turned sideways to look at Jay with fire in her eyes. "You have no business bringing your views into a woman's decision," she said with spite. "Sucked out of the womb? Where in the hell did you…"

"I've told you," Jay said stiffly. "We've been through this, what, a hundred times?" He glanced at his wife for a moment, and then back to the road to prevent sliding into the ditch. "You never did watch that documentary now did you?"

"I don't need to," Elsa said sharply.

"You should," Jay said with conviction. "It discusses all the latest research results; the dangers women encounter from having an abortion; their risk of getting breast cancer. I'd never want you to have an abortion because you'd be a good candidate for getting it—especially with the amount of smoking you do."

"Don't lecture me on smoking."

"You need to quit."

"You need to stop with the lectures," Elsa shot back. "Abortion is a mute subject from here on out. The same goes for my smoking. So just cool it. In fact, just shut up."

"Stop being so dramatic," Jay said calmly but with conviction. "And they are not mute subjects. I'll say whatever I want, when I want, especially when it's the truth."

Elsa didn't want to hear one more word about abortions or the risks of having it done. She took a long pull on her cigarette, turned frontward and sighed deeply. A minute of silence filled the semi's cab, and then Elsa changed the subject after calming

31

down. "My father's a nice man," she said evenly, "He's wanted you to go to work for him for over six months. You have plenty of management skills. He could use you in his store to run things. He needs a man with your wisdom and understanding of business, so he can retire soon."

"He'll never retire."

"What makes you think that?"

"He loves being in control...far too much. He loves the power."

"He's not like that," Elsa replied, defending her father. "He's just a hard working man."

"Another reason why he'll never retire," Jay said firmly. "He wouldn't know what to do with himself. Nor have anyone to order around. Besides, if he did retire, what would he do? He hates golf. Fishing and hunting repulses him."

"He just says that. It just so happens, he's been on several cruises: Carnival, Viking, Holland America, Royal Princess, and the Sea bourn Luxury Cruise Line. Dad's no fool with his money and he always goes for the bargain cruises he's been on with his wife."

"That many, huh," Jay asked with misgivings.

"Well, three that I know of," Elsa said. "They had a good time from what I heard."

"He told me he hated going. He's bitched to me about 'em. So I asked him: why do you go. You know what he said?" Jay didn't wait for Elsa's response. "To save my marriage."

"You're nuts," She said, "He really does want to retire someday."

"Then he can put one of his loyal staff members in charge." Jay said. "Fred Meeks has been with him for what, seventeen years? Thomas Sanders for almost twenty; and Steve—"

"He can't. Elsa interjected, "he doesn't trust them."

"You just made my point," Jay said. "He doesn't trust anyone. That includes me and, believe it or not, he doesn't trust you."

"Me," Elsa replied a bit startled. "Who told you that?"

"He did," Jay said evenly. "He said you love money too much."

"He did not," Elsa exclaimed, feeling stunned and angry at the same time.

"Afraid he did," Jay went on, ignoring his wife's remarks. "and he also believes you'd destroy the business if he put you in charge of it."

Elsa was incensed. "He didn't tell you that," she hissed between clenched teeth. "I know everything there is to know about his business. I mean everything."

"You may know the business, but you don't know how to manage money. That's why men usually hold the purse strings until they know their wives have the financial wherewithal to be good at it. Besides it's the captain that runs the ship babe."

"Screw you," Elsa said, in a malicious voice.

"Take it up with your father. I was just quoting the dear old man. And I was only joking about the last part; that is, for the most part." He snickered.

"I will. And you'd better not be messing with me."

Jay drove on in silence for a good minute, ignoring his wife's last remark. Shortly, when Elsa was about to say something, he started singing: "Some people are born to be tied down; some people are born to be free…"

"Stop singing," Elsa said with scorn.

"Thought you liked Waylon?"

"Waylon Jennings can sing. You flat out can't."

"That bad, huh?"

"Worse," Elsa said almost in a whisper.

Jay raised his voice: "I'LL NEVER SEE TEXAS, L.A., OR OLD MEXICO. DRINKING AND DREAMING…"

"Not now," Elsa shouted above Jay. She put her left hand over her ear. "Stop it!" Jay stopped singing. He grinned and chuckled softly as Elsa went on, repeating her statement about her father. "You just had to change the subject again, huh? Answer me. What's wrong with my father's business?"

"Nothing's wrong with his business. I just don't like working indoors, being tied down in one spot."

"And so you run down the highways."

"Better than being tied down."

"You should consider what I want too, there's more, you're self-centered and full of yourself. My father really does need you. He's told me. In fact on the phone today, he wanted me to…"

"Talk me into giving up my job to work for him," Jay talked over Elsa, completing her sentence.

"Yes. That's what he-"

"Yeah, right," Jay said pointedly. He shook his head slowly as he continued to watch the road. "He'd find something wrong, something missing, and I'd be his perfect scapegoat. He'd send me to jail."

"You're the only one in the family he can trust with his business. How can you think that? He would never have you arrested."

Jay shook his head and brushed her off. "That's a laugh. Since when has he trusted me, let alone anyone?"

"He's always trusted you."

"That's news to me."

"Everything's news to you," she said. She realized she still had the lighter in her hand. She leaned forward and shoved it firmly into its chrome socket. "You know what?" She said, after taking a long pull on her cigarette. "I have an update for you."

"What?" Jay asked. He didn't really care and wondered why he had opened up his big mouth. She was just going to voice a complaint.

"Over two hours," she said with disgust. Jay shook his head; he was right. "Do you hear me? Over two more hours in this——this damn truck is going to drive me up the wall." She moved uneasily in her seat. "You know I have a bad back and this seat just aggravates me." She inhaled deeply and blew a thick cloud of smoke towards Jay.

"Come on," He said, fanning at the smoke. "Knock it off! You know I hate it when you do that!"

"Do what?" She asked, suppressing a grin.

"Blowing smoke in my direction," he said holding his emotions at bay, curtailing his anger. "And *YOU* know it!" He

38

capitalized the word _you_ to underscore his point.

"Would you like it if I just put it out?" Elsa asked, her lips pressed tightly together. "Bother you that much?"

"You know it does. So, put it out! Please!"

"In a bit. I need a little more."

"Then crack your window."

"Is there anything else I can do?" She asked, lowering her window just a little. "Damn, it's freezing out there. Slow down a little."

"Take a pill and relax," he said, and then wished she would take the whole damn bottle. Wow, his last thought sent a shiver up and down his spine; he had never thought such a thing about his wife before. It surprised and scared him at the same time. He swallowed the lump in his throat, and then said: "We'll be in Sandpoint be———"

"You're nuts!" She cut in sharply. "Especially if you think I'm going to crawl back into that bunk. Not on this road. I hate——"

"——driving in this sort of weather," Jay said on top of her irritable tone. He could see her look of anger out of the corner of his eyes. "We wouldn't have to be," he said before she had a chance to speak. "Your father's pretending to be sick again." Jay sighed deeply and slowly moved his head from side-to-side. "It's his way to get you up to see him."

Elsa, silently fuming because Jay had the audacity to mimic her, took another long pull on her Winston and then slowly exhaled the smoke in his direction. "Pretending?" She asked slowly. "He has a heart condition."

"No, he doesn't. I talked with his doctor. It's…"

"You did what?" Elsa asked sharply.

Jay remained calm. "It's stress. He needs to control his blood pressure. His

40

doctor said there's nothing wrong with his heart."

"How could you do that? Did he give you permission?"

"Nope. Just called up to check his story out."

"And they told you? When?"

"Does it matter?"

"Yes, it does."

"A few months ago. After his last urgent plea for us to come up to see him. When we took him to the hospital. The doc said he had a heart of a young bull."

Elsa was speechless. She took another long pull on her cigarette and blew the smoke towards Jay, and then said, "You ass hole," She grunted loudly in disbelief. "You know all about his stress and you refuse to work for him, making up excuses about how much he hates you. You're deplorable."

Jay picked up a note pad from the top of the dash and fanned at the cloud of smoke. "Stop blowing smoke in my face," he demanded.

Elsa ignored his request. "My father's sick!"

"Truth comes out, huh? That's why he wants me to go to work for him."

"He trust you. Think about it."

"I have. And the answer is no, a big fat no."

"This job is going to kill you some day. I don't understand what you———"

"I like what I'm doing," Jay said squarely, cutting Elsa off.

"Why? Cause it takes you away from me?"

"No. It's a good way to make money," Jay paused. "And just like in the song, some are born to be tied down; some are born to be free." He paused and let out a heavy sigh before going on. "I love the freedom of the road." He paused again. "And if you'd give it a chance, you could learn to love it too."

"I've tried. I hate it."

42

"I hate sitting behind a desk," Jay said firmly. "Putting up with office politics is the kind of thing that would kill me." Jay looked at his wife for a moment. "This job makes me a better man. I'm happier and healthier."

"Oh, please," Elsa said with disgust. "You're indifference gives me a headache."

"Indifference," He asked with raised eyebrows. "Since when have I been indifferent?"

"Since the day you quit managing that theatre and took this job!"

"Bull!"

"No, it's not bull," Elsa said, tightlipped. "And you don't give a shit about my family either. You despise every one of them."

"That's not true," He said, shaking his head. "If I was indifferent, I would have stayed home tonight!"

"No, you wouldn't. You had to come up this way. To drop off that load of produce. Then you'd be out on one of your runs. Probably east to Chicago or Atlanta."

"Maybe? You could come with me. Think of it as a vacation. The last time you went across country with me, you said it was a great time."

Elsa sighed deeply and took another long pull on her cigarette, and then coldly said: "I lied. It made me sick."

Jay gripped the steering wheel with both hands as a foreboding silence filled the cab, a silence that gave him an eerie feeling that something was up with Elsa. He stole a quick glance at his wife. She was a medium-sized woman with a curvaceous figure, flaming red hair that curled slightly at her shoulders, and sensitive sea-green eyes; eyes that used to fill his world with love and compassion. But not anymore; now they were filled with derision, hostility, and loathing. He had no idea what it was that she wanted anymore. Elsa never wanted to talk things over. She wanted more than what he could give, and she couldn't care less about his needs. He had tried and tried to appease her wishes, and he had even overlooked her badgering and degrading comments. But enough had been enough; it seemed to Jay that their relationship had run its course. He'd put his foot down a good six months back and ever since things between them had only grown worse.

"We have three cars," Elsa said sharply, bringing him out of his thoughts. "And I don't see why we have to take this——this semi? We could have taken the Blazer."

"Like you said," Jay said squarely, but feeling cornered. "I can drop this load off early and maybe pick up another one before we leave. Why should I make two trips? Besides, we're making money and that's being economical."

"If you get another load out of the Sandpoint area, it will take you east. And

45

then someone will have to drive me back home."

"Your cousin Amy can," Jay said. "She's done it before."

"Her husband won't let her," Elsa said. "He thinks she's seeing someone else. He's watching her like a hawk."

"Is she?" Jay asked.

"If she is, more power to her. Vincent's a nut case."

"Then she should divorce him. Take him to the cleaners."

"You sound like you hate his guts!"

"I don't hate anyone," Jay said. "I just don't have room in my life for certain kinds of people. Vincent drinks too much." Jay paused a moment, shaking his head. "He claims he's fighting the desire to drink but every time we see him, he's drinking. I think he's losing the battle."

"Whatever," Elsa said, and then sighed deeply, "just don't take a load east. I want you to take me home."

"I'll take you home. But only on one condition—if there are no loads available and I need to drive west to pick one up— then I'll drive you home."

"Right," Elsa said with a groan.

"That's the way it must be. It's my job. And if you need your cousin to drive you home, or someone else who's willing, that's how you get back."

"I'd rather rent a car," Elsa said, looking out the window as a light snow began to fall.

"No rentals," Jay said. "Let Amy take you home. There's nothing wrong in that."

"Perhaps," Elsa replied, and then added: "Did you know they dislike it when you pull up in front of the house in this big rig?"

"No one's said anything to me about it."

"It's an insult to me and my family. They hate it when you pull into the
47

neighborhood with this big truck. It's so damn loud, especially when that——that reefer goes on and off all night."

"It was thoughtless of me, I suppose."

"You can say that again," Elsa replied.

"Well, if it makes you feel any better, I'll apologize to everyone and park at the truck stop."

"What truck stop?" She insisted.

"We've been through this," Jay said, feeling edgy. "Give it a rest!"

"What truck stop?" Elsa asked again, ignoring her husband's remarks.

"The one up on Highway Two," Jay said as he glanced over at his wife, "across the road from the new Wal-Mart. I'll drop you off and then take it over and park it. I can walk back."

"That's over a mile away," Elsa said.

"I promise not to complain," Jay replied.

"It's still an embarrassment."

"Sorry. But you know we're up to our ears in debt. We have a second mortgage and credit cards to pay off. I can't do it driving a car or an SUV."

"Why do you always bring up credit cards? You never say anything about a truck payment when you discuss bills. Why is that? Do you think I'm stupid? I know what you're really saying. If it wasn't for what I've done to make our home look nice, we wouldn't have all those bills."

"I wasn't thinking about any of that," Jay said abruptly, cutting his wife off. "I told you why we're taking the truck and that's all."

"I doubt it," Elsa said cuttingly.

"It would be nice if you'd consider our economic situation be——"

"There you go again," she cut in, "using that word, economics. I swear you must be in love with that word."

"You should be too."

"Please," She said with a sardonic look.

49

"Think before you buy." That's all I'm suggesting," he replied.

"What? Think before I buy? You think I'm stupid or what?" Elsa asked, releasing a cloud of smoke from her lungs.

"You're not stupid."

"Make me a believer," Elsa said, daring him.

"Just ask yourself if we really need that tasteless piece of junk." That really ticked off Elsa to the core, which he wasn't trying to do.

"Junk?" Elsa cried out, making her statement into a question; her eyes wide open with rage. "You're insulting me on purpose. There's nothing wrong with my taste."

"It's not so much your taste. It's the price you pay for—everything. You've got no sense when it comes to money."

"You've got to be kidding," Elsa was furious, knowing full well that he was dead serious. In fact, whenever money was involved, Jay was a man of debits and credits, debits and credits. And everything, including her checking account, had to balance on a weekly basis. Which in reality, if he didn't take care of her accounts, they would be in the poorhouse. "You said that 'cause my father thinks that, huh?"

"I'm not kidding," Jay said slowly, ignoring her remark about her father.

"That's the trouble. You're too serious."

"Think before you buy," Jay said firmly.

"There you go," Elsa said, crossing her arms in front of her. "You're in love with that word, E-C-O-N-O-M-I-C-S!" She spoke every letter with contempt.

"Well do me a favor. From now on——don't buy anything without discussing it with me first. Okay?"

51

"What about my comfort--do you ever stop to consider how I feel?" She whined like a six year old spoiled child.

"All the time. You just don't notice."

"What's to notice?" She whimpered.

"Quite a bit."

"Such as?"

"What we've been discussing for one thing. Which reminds me? Stop buying all those magazines; and cancel your subscriptions to the ones you no longer read. Throw them out, they clutter up the bedroom."

"I'm keeping them," Elsa said defensively. "Anything else on your mind?"

"Our marriage," Jay replied. "We could use some help in that arena. We need counseling."

"Out of the question," Elsa said with the air of a threat. "Only idiots seek counseling. Idiots who expect to change their partners, to mold them into something

52

they can never be—or want to be. We don't need counseling."

"Counseling helps," Jay was firm about the issue on counselors, "if you give it a chance."

"You're calling yourself an idiot," was her response.

"Don't be silly." Jay was growing weary of this whole road trip. "You're seeing a shrink and——"

"Precisely why we don't need to see one. They just sit and listen and give you pills. They're worthless. And so is their counsel. The only thing I've gotten out of it is a prescription for Valium."

Jay dimmed his lights to oncoming traffic. "We have a lot of problems. Problems that need to be addressed."

"Such as?"

"Such as your decision to not have any children."

"We've talked about that," she said firmly, and then shook her left hand fiercely. The pinky ring on her left little finger became active, sending sharp electrical impulses through her body. She moaned and shook her hand violently; not understanding why every time they discussed children or babies the ring would send electrical pulses into her finger. When the small, painful electrical surges stopped, she messaged her hand on her leg and quickly said: "My decision will never change. Never." She was emphatic about not having children.

"What was that all about? What's wrong with your hand?"

"Nothing's wrong. Just drop the subject."

"I can't. We need to talk this out with——"

"I don't need anyone telling me how I feel. Especially another four eyed, nerdish shrink who charges a hundred and sixty dollars an hour. I'm not crazy, I'm just going through some changes," Elsa defiantly stated.

"We need to do something." Jay quietly suggested.

"Why, because you need," she hesitated, hoping the ring would not hurt her again, "children and I don't?" No electrical charges came. Elsa sighed in relief.

"And why is that? You———"

"I've told you," Elsa said sharply, cutting him off. "My mother died giving birth to me. And my father, for the first sixteen years of my life, hated me. I had to live with my Aunt Rita until she died. And that was a living hell. She hated me as much as my father did."

"Then why do you run every time he calls?"

"You can be so lame," Elsa said with a condescending look. "What's done is done. People change. It's that simple."

"He put you in his will, didn't he?"

55

Elsa pulled hard on her cigarette. "Just get me up to Sandpoint, okay? And drop the subject about children. I don't want children. Is that clear?" Again the ring did not send electrical jolts into her sore finger. Maybe that was it; her finger could only take so much pain. She glanced at her finger that was slightly tender. She was completely perplexed about the ring and why it seemed to attack her at times.

Jay interrupted her thoughts: "We really should sit down with someone and discuss this."

Elsa felt the hairs on the nape of her neck rise. "I said I don't want to go on with the conversation," She said, tightlipped. "Didn't you hear me say that?"

"I heard you," Jay said firmly.

"Nothing's going to change my mind about having children. And don't tell me we don't communicate because we just did!" Elsa was certain about not having kids and it really riled her when Jay brought the subject up.

"We don't communicate. We just grunt and huff and puff!" Jay flicked his headlights back on high beam.

"Oh my, like the three little pigs?" Elsa said smugly. "I do believe I've touched a nerve. It doesn't surprise me. You're just like your father. You expect me to be a mother and your kitchen slave. You can't stand it when I ask you to fix dinner. The kitchen is my domain, right?" Jay remained silent, not wanting to hear this argument again. "I think maybe we should get a divorce."

"What?" Jay asked, somewhat annoyed.

"A divorce. A D-I-V-"

"I heard you," He blared.

"O-R-C-E," She went on, her eyes blazing with scorn.

"Like I said the last time you brought it up," Jay said evenly as his hands griped the

57

steering wheel a lot tighter. "You can have it all——the house, the cars...and the bills!"

"I don't think so. I have no income. I don't work. The judge will be sure to side with me."

"I doubt that. Not if I bring those two affairs into it."

"You would, wouldn't you," She asked scornfully—yet at the same time a bit ashamed and scared?

"Tit for tat," Jay said flatly. He paused briefly, not wanting to go any further with the discussion. "You could go back to work for Safeway," he interjected to change the subject. "With an income you could help pay off our bills."

"You're a hypocrite," Elsa almost murmured the words.

"You're an adulteress," he replied firmly.

Dead silence filled the cab. Elsa's lips quivered as she puffed on her cigarette and looked through the right side window into the dark cold terrain. The trees were covered with snow and she wondered how much more the branches of the evergreens could withstand before they were forced to bend downward or snap? She also wondered how much more she could put up with before she snapped, before she wound up in someone's arms again. It was the loneliness, she had explained to Jay, as the reason for her affairs. But that wasn't the whole truth. The truth was that she couldn't stand Jay anymore. She hated everything about him, especially the fact that he used words that she didn't understand. She was jealous of his speech and felt that because he was merely a truck driver, he should stay in his station. He even did crossword puzzles in ink. Just who did he think he was, showing off like that? She'd had enough and she wanted out and she knew that a divorce was most likely not an option at this point; thanks to her two affairs; divorce would not be the right avenue of escape. She would lose everything. The judge would have no sympathy, none whatsoever for an adulteress. She was trapped and felt homicidal. She could kill the person who had told Jay about her affairs——that is, if she knew who it was.

"You stress me out with your obsessions, Elsa said coldly, breaking the silence. "Almost as bad as Phyllis Keating, that slut my father's taken up with."

"I thought you liked her?" Jay chided after a silent moment.

"I can't stand the witch. She's trailer trash with a dirty mouth. No one likes her. She's only seven years older than I am, and she's always talking a mile a minute."

"Hey, hey, hey, she's not that bad." We were looking for a double wide ourselves last summer. Don't talk like that; it's not flattering."

60

"She's a nut case," Elsa said sharply, eyeing her husband with impertinence. "Did you hear what she had her bratty kid do last summer?"

"I heard," Jay interjected, then inhaled a slow breath through his nose and let it right back out in one burst, to relieve the pounding pressure in his head.

Elsa went on griping, "that woman allowed her little brat to be lowered down head first with just a rope tied around his ankles to fetch a wallet his uncle had somehow lost in that old outhouse they use from time-to-time." Elsa just kept on a roll without taking a breath, about the story of Phyllis's boy, which made her stomach start to growl. "Phyllis made her son sound as if he were some sort of saint, after he was tied up with a rope and lowered head first into that spider-infested stink hole. I can just imagine what he must have smelled like when he found the filthy wallet and they

61

pulled him back up." Elsa cringed and shook herself out, acting as if she was swiping at flies with both hands.

By this time, Jay was emotionally drained and gripped the steering wheel so tight that his knuckles turned white, (which didn't go unnoticed by Elsa). He wished she would take a pill. Boy they were two prize fighters. He followed the road as it curved a little to the west, down into a wide ravine and then under a structured railroad trestle that was inundated with a thick blanket of fog. Coming out of the fog bank, he drove out of the ravine and then, within the blink of an eye, a large yellow road sign suddenly materialized on the right side of the road. It had two amber lights flashing brightly, lights that resembled the eyes of a large medieval dragon. The lights created unusual patterns and mysterious shadows on the icy road and snow packed tundra. Its unexpected appearance gave Jay a start. He gasped loudly and almost jackknifed the truck by jerking the wheel too much to the left. He over corrected his mistake too fast and this created a nightmarish ride on the unexpected black ice. Elsa's nerve-racking screams filled the truck as Jay fought for control, veering to the right and to the left and to the right and to the left as his mind screamed: KEEP YOUR FOOT OFF THE BRAKE!

"WHAT'S WRONG WITH YOU?" Elsa yelled furiously, wide-eyed and shaking after Jay had regained control of the truck and trailer and pulled to the side of the road. "YOU TRYING TO KILL US OR WHAT?"

Jay, who had no conception of physics——or the desire to understand the science——wiped the cold sweat from his brow, grateful to have survived the frightening and spasmodic calamity. He also felt stupid and somewhat embarrassed. He was supposed to be an experienced driver, a professional who doesn't panic over road signs. (In actuality, he didn't panic. His subconscious took over and expertly navigated them through the impossible nightmare.) Stunned but calmed, he took a deep breath and let it out slowly, feeling sweat ooze from every pore of his six-foot frame. Tickling as it dribbled down his sides from his armpits. "It's okay," he said, feeling his heart beating hard and fast against his chest. "I just lost———"

"You could have killed us," Elsa cut in sharply, but not as loud. "Or we could be in a ditch right now with no hope of getting out alive. We'd freeze in this damn truck and then the wild animals would have their way with us. I sure hope you realize that."

"Please, Pidge. I know———"

"Stop calling me Pidge!" Elsa cried in disgust, with her face twisted up in both emotional and physical pain, "I hate that name!" She picked up her cigarette that had fallen on the floor and made sure the carpet wasn't smoldering. "I'm not your little

64

pigeon! God, I feel as if I've aged twenty years," she went on nagging like it was her second language, putting out the half-smoked cigarette in the ashtray. "Thanks to that crazy stunt you just pulled, I've lost all my confidence in your driving. And you call yourself a professional. What a joke that is!"

Jay ignored his wife's ranting as he regained his composure. When his breathing had returned to normal and his heart no longer felt as if it were trying to rip out of his chest, he began to study the area around the mysterious road sign through his right rear view mirror. The sign's flashing lights continued to create eerie shadows throughout the area. But it wasn't so much the sign that disturbed him. It was what the sign had said:

SPOUSE DISPOSAL SITE
27 MILES

It had to be some sort of joke, Jay thought, as he massaged the tightness out of the back of his neck. That was the only logical explanation behind its presence. Someone had placed the sign up as a joke. And that someone had turned it on just as soon as he had driven out of the foggy ravine.

Jay began searching the shadows alongside the road for any sign of movement, hoping he was right and the sign was nothing more than a college prank. "Spouse Disposal Site", he pondered with a skeptical snort, who in their right mind would believe in such a place?

"Talk to me, Jay!" Elsa demanded for the third time, nudging him on the arm. "What's wrong with you? What's going on?" Not that she cared; she was just concerned for her own wellbeing.

"It's that sign," he replied slowly, avoiding his wife's frightened eyes. "Did you see it?"

Elsa glanced at the rear view mirror on her side of the cab, "I see it. What about it?"

"What did it say? Did you read it?" He asked.

"Something about snow plows," she answered with a shrug. "Why?"

"Snow plows? Are you sure?"

"Of course I'm sure. I'm not blind. She squirmed in her seat, watching her husband's inquiring eyes search from side-to-side. "Go take a look if you don't believe me," she said. "You have two legs."

"I might do just that," he replied hoarsely, thinking he saw some movement off to the right as a gust of wind shook the truck.

"What did you think the sign said," Elsa asked? She took a cigarette from her almost empty pack of Winston's.

"I know this may sound a little ludicrous," he said slowly, as he continued to observe the shadows beyond the truck. "I

67

could swear it said something about a Spouse Disposal Site."

"A what," Elsa asked after swallowing a lump in her throat?

"A Spouse Disposal Site—about 27 miles up the road," Walter replied as he continued to look through his rear view mirrors.

Elsa shoved the lighter back into its chrome socket. "You're crazy, she said, and then thought to herself: just what I need to start anew—a place to get rid of Walter. The answer was just ahead; fate was intervening to aid in her escape. "What a crackpot," she said between pressed lips, "You're as bad as that loon in Sandpoint. Maybe you and Phyllis should sit down and compare notes."

"I'm not crazy," Jay said with a short pause, "believe me."

"Then get us off the side of the road. We're going to be late if we just sit here. Then she nervously lit her cigarette as a sense of Deja vu swept through her. "And you know how my father can be."

"I don't care how your father can be. I want to look at that sign."

"Forget the damn sign," Elsa demanded, and pursed her lips angrily together. "Let's just get off the side of this icy road. I need to use the restroom." She shuddered uncontrollably as another feeling of Déjà vu hit her, this time with a vignette of some big creature of a man poking at her midsection with a silver object. She was lying on a hospital bed, covered with a white sheet; bright lights shone from above. And the man's eyes were as dark as night, almost reptilian. Elsa shuddered again as the vision quickly past.

Jay watched his wife squirm uneasily in her seat for a few moments and then, after she gave him a puffed-up and intense gaze, slowly eased back onto the highway, wishing he had taken a few minutes to go back and look at the sign. But then, he would have never heard the last of it. Elsa would have nagged him all the way to her father's house if he had gone back to take a second glimpse at the sign. He watched it slowly disappear in his rear view mirror, and thought again that it had to be a hoax, placed there by some frat kids who had nothing better to do than to try and scare the wits out of people as they drove past.

"You're not talking. What are you thinking about?" Elsa asked a few miles later, trying to draw Jay back into another confrontation. "That stupid sign back there"?

Jay eased up on the accelerator as he crossed a small icy bridge. "No, he said briefly, not liking the way Elsa's cold, calculating eyes, like an old hand held can opener, seemed to pry the lid off his soul. "But I take it you have?" Man, why did I say that? Here we go again, he thought.

"I don't need to," she smugly replied, "I know it was just your crazy imagination running amuck again."

70

Jay reached over and flicked on the radio. When it came on and he glanced over at Elsa, he could tell she didn't like what was on. He asked in a lighter tone if she wanted to hear something else, but she remained silent. She was now giving him the cold shoulder, and by refusing to answer, she'd be the martyr. If she did say that Jay should change it, she'd be the bitch. So it was the martyr for now, till she figured out a different strategy. Jay knew it and waited, resting his nerves in the deadening silence that exploded into a rebuke on him even though there was music playing. After what seemed like an eternity, Jay finally broke with tradition and the usual same old, same old battle cycle, which he found himself snared in once again with this woman that he'd tried so faithfully to love. But now he wasn't sure of what to do, or why this was all happening to them. He just knew some things needed a higher power to fix—what wasn't humanly possible. Jay took the high road and turned off the radio like a gentleman and said, "Let's just finish what we were discussing and see if we can save the day. So, what was the subject? Ah, yes, my foolish emotions; emotions that you have no doubt, come to loathe." He picked up speed again, feeling confused; stuck between a rock and a hard spot.

"Among other things," Elsa said callously.

"Such as," He asked? "I give up."

"Such as your selfish and inconsiderate attitude, your childish pranks, and your suspicions. You're a foolish man and I'm sick of it."

"So what's your solution? It seems the goodness in your soul has died," Jay said, sadly. "That soft, delicate soul that I tried so hard to nurture with love and understanding has become dark—like a swamp; like a murky river of wretchedness."

72

"That's right", Elsa said smugly, "you've taken the life right out of me. Thanks to you and your irresponsible plans and ideas about love. You make it hard for me to breathe."

"To breathe," Jay questioned? "What are you—who are you?"

"You question every move I make", Elsa said harshly; ignoring his questions. "I feel like I'm drowning."

"It's your own doing", he pushed back.

"Forgive and forget". Elsa dryly commented.

"You feeling guilty," Jay asked? He was on it now and wanted to provoke some human response from her.

"What's that supposed to mean?" Elsa asked.

"God knows I've tried to love you Elsa."

"Not very hard," Elsa snapped. "You've never had what it takes to make me happy," she said with a tone set in cement.

"So…um…so, there's just no pleasing you, huh? You feel guilty because you're already setting up the stage for another fling; right?"

"You're nothing but a lame, broken down old horse that ain't even worth shoeing. And you're right, whatever you say."

With that, Jay was crushed and his heart felt the blow. Like the ox, knowing it was almost at the end of a long winding road, he had to regain his courage and haul this heavy load on its final journey over the highest mountains and through the deepest darkest dales. No reprieve now.

"Astrologically speaking," Jay said, "you're the horse. And I'm the Ox," he said defensively. "And I want this whole damn nightmare to stop."

"What," Elsa asked harshly?

"I said you're the horse. The Fire Horse, that's your sign."

"You're sick," she cried, trying to feign tears to garner sympathy to get out of the deep water she suddenly found herself in.

"Actually, In Chinese Astrology, you were born in the year of the Fire Horse," Jay went on, ignoring his wife's remark, "which means that your parents probably would have killed you? Due to the belief that all girls born under your sign are too much like a horse on fire, too hard to control, too hard to tame or train. They always bring the family shame or grief because of their audacious outspoken traits."

"You've got to be kidding?" Elsa was nervous and stunned.

"I'm serious." Jay glanced at his wife. He returned his gaze to the road and smiled. "They really did kill the baby girls that were born during that year—and by the thousands."

"That's enough."

"Perhaps they still do?" Jay went on.

"All right Jay. That's enough. I don't want to hear any more about it. Nothing!"

"Why? Feel a little uneasy?"

"It insults me. It's nothing but a pack of cruel superstition and nonsense."

"There's no nonsense about it," Jay said. He looked at his wife with a grin. Elsa felt a bit trapped and disconcerting. Of course she knew all about the history of Chinese Astrology and knew she was indeed a fire-horse, but she did not want to be dissected as one. She ran her right hand through her thick luxurious hair and studied Jay's hideous grin with contempt.

"Watch the damn road," she said harshly. "You're driving off the road!" Jay turned his attention back to the road while Elsa considered her situation; a change of subject was needed.

"You ever have an affair," Elsa asked?

"It's a science." Jay continued to go on about the Fire Horse; ignoring her question of infidelity.

"Forget your stupid mumbo-jumbo science. Answer me. Did you ever—"

"Never," Jay said firmly, cutting her off.

"I find that hard to believe."

Jay glanced sideways at his wife. "Yah, I know you do because fidelity is something you can't do—so I'm not surprised," he said, then breathed deeply. "Shifting gears again?"

She ignored the question and tried to keep a poker face yet her bewilderment was over the top.

"I know", Jay said evenly. "My feelings really don't mean a damn thing to you anymore, now do they?"

Elsa grumbled as she opened her window and flicked her cigarette into the cold night. "Forget how I feel," she said, in a tough cranky voice, rolling her window back up. "Just get us to Sandpoint in one piece." She picked up her purse from the floor and removed her small brown plastic bottle of Valiums. She placed two of the yellow tranquilizers on her tongue, swallowed them dry, and then put the bottle back inside her handbag, letting it drop back down on the floor with a thud.

Jay, watching her from the corner of his eyes, felt a tinge of compassion for her. "You'd be better off in the bunk, he said softly. "Stretch out and get some sleep."

"No thanks! It's like a coffin back there."

"Really," Jay asked. He let out a low grunt, and then added: "Never thought of it in those terms."

"To me it is. And I don't feel like bouncing up and down and sideways till I fall asleep. It would drive me nuts."

"Suit yourself," Jay said, slowly bobbing his head from side-to-side, like he was trying to juggle the moment mentally.

78

"But you really would be more comfortable sleeping back there instead of dosing off in that seat. The road's not that bad."

"Just find me a bathroom, okay?"

"That bad, eh?"

"Bad enough."

"Can you wait about ten minutes or so," He asked?

Elsa leaned back in her seat and released a deep sigh. She wasn't a happy camper before, but now this was making her steaming mad. She gave Jay a look that could kill. While distraught over the fact that this guy, who was her husband, was a dolt and that she now felt nothing for her once upon a time knight in shining armor, she closed her eyes and tried to recall just what it was about him that she'd liked so much to marry him. Nothing came to mind. Her thoughts turned to the little ring on her finger. She started to rotate it slowly and scenes flashed for a brief moment in her mind. They made little sense to her. She tried to remove it again, but the band of gold seemed to shrink when she tried, as it always had before. She frowned as she looked down at the ring and gave up trying to remove it.

"I'm an idiot," she mumbled, as she faced forward to watch the winter's night slip past while waiting for the tranquilizer's to kick in.

"What?"

"I said I can wait, as she glanced at Jay, then closed her eyes saying, "Just slow down a bit. The road's icy."

"It's been plowed and sanded. We'll be okay."

"Just the same, slow down."

Jay ignored his wife's request to take it slow. He was done in by the useless fighting, so he slipped one of his Donovan CD's into the player and turned up the volume just enough to hear the music, hoping Elsa wouldn't complain. She hated his music. If it wasn't country, it wasn't music, as far as she was concerned. Because of the shrillness of her voice, that was worse than the sound of grating fingernails on a chalk board, his thoughts turned dark. He thought of the sign and wondered if he could really murder his wife. The thought frightened him. It had never crossed his mind before——that is, until tonight when they had come across the eerie sign. But, he reasoned, as he drove on through the frigid night with Donovan singing "Season of The Witch", there's a first time for everything.

At that moment another road sign with amber lights was just ahead. Jay slowed down a bit and from the corner of his eyes he watched the sign and Elsa. A few seconds after passing the sign he asked his wife if she had read it. Again she replied that it was nothing but a warning about being aware of snow plows working the highway and to use extreme caution. But that wasn't true. He had read it himself. It was another sign stating there was indeed a Spouse Disposal Site not far ahead. Either he was imagining what it said or she had lied again. He could feel a sense of mistrust and loathing in the cab; along with a renewed sense of curiosity. And if there was any validity behind the mysterious road signs, perhaps tonight would be the night to seek out and use the services of the Spouse Disposal Site.

* * *

Two

Jay pulled his tractor-trailer up in front of the old weathered building, made of mud brick which had the look of ancient origins from times past and shut off the truck's lights but left the diesel engine running by placing the unit into optimized idle to keep the fuel from jelling. The dwelling, which resembled a Swiss chalet with a wide overhang on both ends, and a porch that ran along the entire length of the building, sat in a dark cul-de-sac near the base of a huge mountain. Rustic, wooden tables and chairs were piled close together on the far side of the porch, along with a faded neon sign that advertised the place as a 24 hour diner, which made it appear as though the chalet had been here for quite some time, yet Jay had trouble recalling the establishment, let alone the roadside entrance leading up to the eatery.

The cry of a lone wolf in the distance, along with the thin streaks of moonlight filtering through the low gray clouds and lofty firs, sent a creepy shiver through his entire body. The haunting call of loons coming off the nearby lake gave him a feeling that they were being observed from the changing shadows that surrounded the mysterious enterprise. He swallowed the lump of fear, tightening in his throat and

massaged the back of his neck, which felt like a noose had been slipped over his head. When he grasped what he was doing—trying to scare himself into leaving the area and getting back on the highway, he laughed quietly at the ridiculous thoughts racing through his mind.

"What's so funny," Elsa asked?

Jay glanced at his wife and knew she was also somewhat apprehensive about climbing out of the truck and entering the diner.

"Nothing," he said.

"Since when do you laugh at nothing?"

"I don't. It's just that I felt someone was watching us, from that large window." Jay pointed to the center window with large thick curtains. "Looks like the drapes were pulled apart a little bit."

"So, you laugh," Elsa asked with a hint of amusement? She sighed deeply, and then asked: "What did you expect? If anyone's in there, they'd notice your big rig pulling into their parking lot. I'd look to see who it was too. You paranoid?"

"No, I'm not," Jay replied.

"We going in or what," Elsa demanded after a moment of silence?

"I suppose," Jay answered with a shrug. "You do have to use the ladies room, remember?"

Elsa gave Jay the raised eyebrow and smirk look. "Just make sure you leave a tip tonight."

"I always leave tips."

"Don't give me that. You hardly ever leave a tip."

"I will tonight." Jay smiled at his wife. "And it's going to be a big one. That I can promise."

"Make sure you do. It's cheap and disrespectful when you don't. It wouldn't surprise me to hear you've left a poor waitress a penny at times."

"That's an insult. I've…"

"Give her a big tip," Elsa interjected, cutting Jay off. "Don't embarrass me."

Jay climbed out of the truck and slammed the door in Elsa's face, wishing he could shut her mouth just as easily and just as quickly. But maybe I can, he thought, as he held on to the side of the truck to keep from falling on the thin ice. Maybe one can actually dispose of one's spouse in this weird place? His eyes narrowed and a perverse grin spread across his face. And if that sign was really what I thought it was, I could possibly be free within the hour. Jay was startled by his unusual thoughts. Another chilling shudder shot through every fiber of his being; he questioned his sense of morals knowing this entire act of disposing of one's wife must be some sort of test and wasn't necessary. The courts could and would take care of it for him. He stopped and looked at the building and surroundings again; he was about to change his mind and leave--but Elsa opened her door and started berating him in her angry high-pitched voice for taking his time. Okay, he thought, curiosity must be satisfied.

He helped his unsuspecting wife from the truck and up the snow-packed sidewalk to the entrance, fully aware of the two grotesquely looking gargoyles———with their blood-shot eyes and wolf-like spouts——— inanimately watching their every step from their protruding and heraldic positions above the door. Two of evil's beastly servants, he thought, as a cold steady wind murmured hauntingly through the tall conifers that surrounded the chalet. The dark winter's clouds were parting to reveal a blue full moon breaking through the thick tree limbs and branches to light up the area. Jay thought it was the perfect scenario to remind all those who step across the threshold of this dimly lit place that they must dig deep within them to find the wicked courage to go through with their grim intentions.

They climbed the steps and he opened the door to the restaurant and stepped inside. They both jumped a bit when the door closed itself with a clanking thud.

We're trapped within the abyss, Jay thought to himself. Within the eerie and dark world of the unknown, we must continue to feed upon curiosity's ugly head. His senses told him some unearthly presence was lurking about, but just what it might be was beyond him. It had to be his nerves, his fear of the unknown, which he had had since he was a young boy. Whatever it was that was making his skin crawl, he knew he had to move forward and face it head on with courage to overcome the unimaginable horror that stands now as part of the chaos in which we have willingly entered.

"What chaos?" A voice within his mind asked.

"The chaos in one's own soul," Jay mumbled softly as he studied the entrance and the door.

"Find us a booth near the window," Elsa said, nudging him out of his thoughts. "I'll be right back."

Jay sat down at the second red booth just to the right of the entrance while Elsa quickly found the ladies room. Jay observed the signs and the fixtures in the restaurant, which surprised and disappointed him at the same time. It wasn't exactly the sort of diner one would expect to find along the highways of America, but it did have all the amenities, including——at the far end of the narrow room———an antiquated jukebox with soft blinking lights. An uplifting but soothing instrumental jazz selection he had never heard before was coming from its one and only speaker; and to its left, near the door to the restrooms, sat a cigarette machine with an 'out of order' sign fastened above the coin slot. Small chandeliers hanging from the ceiling over each booth provided the soft lighting for the room. Just to his left was the restaurant's small counter with the kitchen area directly behind it. The smell of coffee lingered strongly in the room, but that was all. There was no hint of food having ever been cooked in the place, not even the smell of bacon or eggs, steaks, or potatoes, or soups: just the strong aroma of coffee.

Upon Elsa's return, a waitress entered the room from the kitchen, a woman that amazingly resembled Elsa in every way, from her flaming red hair to her shapely legs. Jay studied the woman and felt as though he had just stepped back in time, a little over three years to be exact, to The Yellow Rose, a country and western lounge in Moscow, Idaho, where he had first met Elsa. This is amazing, Jay thought, as the waitress moved down the counter and picked up two coffee mugs and the pot of steaming coffee, she even walks like Elsa. She could be her twin sister——that is, if Elsa had a sister? But she just had two older and mean spirited brothers who were both serving long sentences in Idaho's state penitentiary for growing and selling pot on their small ranch a few miles north of Sandpoint.

The waitress crossed the room and smiled warmly at Jay. Her pink and white uniform clung tightly to her curvaceous figure, and Jay found it extremely difficult to take his eyes off the woman's feminine attributes. He blushed and blinked his eyes at Elsa when the waitress gave him a wink. But Elsa had not seen the flirtation. She was too busy digging through her purse for a book of matches.

The waitress sat the cups on the table and began to pour the hot liquid into them. "How would you like your coffee?" she asked sweetly.

"Cream, I take cream," Jay replied nervously, forcing himself to keep his eyes on the cup in front of him, "no sugar."

"Black," Elsa said stiffly, as she continued to search through her purse.

The waitress removed a small container from her apron. "Try this," she said pleasantly, handing the cream to Jay. "It's the best coffee creamer in the world. I say that because my boss, the owner of this dump, makes it himself." She gave Jay another wink. He quickly peeled back the top of the round container and, feeling shy from the woman's admiration, poured the entire contents into his cup. "You been here long," Jay asked, as he began to stir his coffee?

"About two years," She replied. "We don't do much business in winter. Summer's our busiest time."

"What's your name?"

"Pidge," the redhead said softly, "I'll be your waitress," she said demurely, knowing the sound of her name had disturbed Jay. She gave Jay another wink when he glanced up at her with his mouth open. "If you need anything, just call."

"I'd like a book of matches," Elsa demanded, giving up her search for a light. She looked at the waitress for the first time and merely gestured to Pidge with a wave of her hand that held an unlit cigarette between her fingers; her nails were coated with a light shade of red to highlight her hair.

Pidge removed a book of matches from the pocket of her apron and gave them to Elsa, who took them without uttering a word of thanks.

"Is there anything else?" Pidge asked, looking down at Elsa with condescension.

"Would you," Jay cleared his throat, "happen to know the name of that song," He asked Pidge?

"Do you like it?" She answered.

"I can't stand it," Elsa hissed while striking a match. "If it ain't country—it ain't music."

"Yes, I do," Jay replied somewhat nervously, after giving his wife a stern look for her unnecessary remark. He glanced up at their waitress. "It's a nice song, melodic."

"I believe that one is C-Smooth, by George Benson." She cooed warmly. "I like it myself. Makes me feel peaceful and—— and romantic." She smiled warmly and took in a deep breath that lifted and showcased her bountiful breasts.

"Oh, Gawd," Elsa moaned. "Give me a break!"

"I'll be back shortly to take your orders," Pidge said, giving Elsa a butterfly

94

glance before moving effortlessly across the room, shaking her tail feathers, knowing Jay was watching and admiring her every step.

Elsa inhaled deeply on her cigarette. "What are you looking at?" She asked with a tough snarl, sharply, eyeing Jay jealously. Elsa didn't want him anymore, but she sure didn't want anybody else to have him either.

"She looks a lot like you," Jay said, turning his gaze from the waitress to Elsa. "You could be sisters."

Elsa glanced at the waitress and then returned her irritable scrutiny to Jay. "In your dreams," she replied with revulsion.

"What's your problem? You———"

"You're my problem, she fired through clenched teeth. I saw the way you were looking at her---with those hideous bedroom eyes of yours. It's disgusting!"

"I don't have bedroom eyes."

Elsa laughed. "Bull. After watching you I know you've been having affairs of your own. Probably three or four--as much time that you spend out on the road. You must have had at least one or two affairs. And don't tell me different."

"That's not true," Jay said defensively.

"I bet you have a waitress, or some bimbo receptionist in shipping and receiving where you deliver and pick up loads. And they can't wait to see you again, to satisfy your loneliness with degrading sexual acts. And they all look just like me. Just like that waitress, huh?"

"She does look like you. Look again and tell me she doesn't. Go on, look."

"I can't," Elsa said. "She's no longer in the room."

"When she comes back, you'll notice."

"Between the two of us, you've looked enough to last us a year, maybe two." Elsa took another hard drag on her cigarette, and then exhaled the smoke--like a slap in Jay's face. "Go ahead and tell me. How many other women look like me?"

"I don't have any," Jay said warily. "And just because I was observing this waitress doesn't mean—"

"Oh paw-lease" she scowled, just-Stop while you're ahead."

Jay leaned on the table, leaning into her to make a private point, trying to get through to her, he said again firmly: "Believe me--I don't sleep around on you, babe. So take your sick mind out of the gutter."

"Sure you do," Elsa said gruffly.

"No I don't," Jay said strongly, defending his veracity.

Elsa furrowed her brows together and patted her eyelashes delicately, as if she were holding back pain filled tears, sniffing them back to prevent a full blown crying jag. Of course she couldn't pull it off; she'd over played it as usual. By trying to play the suffering saint, Elsa overplayed her hand.

"All men do," She moaned, shrugging one shoulder and pouting her lower lip looking all around trying to avert direct contact with Jay's unimpressed gaze until he finally lowered his weary head. Elsa had to change her strategy quickly. She nervously drew in a relieving breath of air and sighed heavily, as if to regain her composure in order to take back the upper hand.

"I don't cheat!" Jay said emphatically in a firm, lowered voice, quietly hitting the table firmly with a powerfully clenched fist. His huge shoulders took on the characteristics of an ox and he looked directly into her eye's through dark impending brows warning her that he was ready to charge because he'd reached the end of his patience, breathing hotly in and out through his fiercely flared nostrils with a slightly insane grimace that exposed a chilling Jack Palance grin, showing his tight jaw and clenched teeth through tightly drawn, turned in lips.

Though cautious, she blew him off saying, "Ah, give it a break. Don't lie to me. All men think about sex constantly and you're no different from all the rest. You're a pervert."

Jay drew back and relaxed his demeanor, knowing full well that he would never hit a woman. He never had and despite the desire to smack Elsa, he wasn't about to start now, no matter how hard she tried to provoke him; no matter how many names she flung into his face. He wasn't going to strike her.

"What is it with you? When a man admires a beautiful woman, a work of art, it's because she's one of nature's rare wonders of the world." He paused to study Elsa's eyes; eyes that were not believing a word he was saying; eyes that were filled with scorn and contempt. "That's why I wanted to marry you Pidge, you're beautiful. I fell in love with you, hard."

"Don't give me that line," Elsa said with a bitter hiss. "It's not true. You don't love me. How could you say that? You're gone too damn long." Elsa didn't want to hear any more about his love for her. She wanted out.

"It's not a line. What's bothering you lately?"

"Why can't you just come out and say you want to have sex with other women? In fact, I know you do. I saw how you were looking at that waitress a few minutes ago. You desire her, don't you? Come out and admit it. You want her body, Jay. You're a sex fiend. Why give me all that hogwash about art and compliments?" She didn't want to hear Jay's feelings, let alone his irritating voice. What she wanted to do was drift back into her fantasy of having her perfect and wealthy man.

"I've seen a lot of men checking you out and it doesn't bug me. In fact it's a compliment."

"So you look and desire other women because men check me out all the time? I

100

know it. That gives you the right to look around too?"

"Stop with this. I don't desire other women," he said defensively, feeling as if his back was up against the wall. "And I've never slept with another woman. That is, since we've been married."

"Your eyes tell me another story Jay."

"I do, at times, like to admire them. That I admit. Especially those who have qualities that stands out in a crowd." Jay paused to take a sip of his coffee. "I don't know," Jay said with a shrug, "maybe it's the "IT" thing that some woman have. Like you. You're truly a work of art. Nature has treated you well." Jay took a long sip of his coffee while Elsa inhaled deeply on her Winston, basking in the sun of the compliments that made her muse on how she was going to use her feminine wiles to land herself a prince charming. "She was right about the cream,"

Jay said, glancing across the table at Elsa. "You should try it."

"Don't change the subject. You're imagining things if you think I'm going to believe that stuff you just told me. You lust after women. It's in your eyes. I've seen you look at those pornographic books your friends, Al and Sara have in their basement. And don't try to deny it." She blew another puff of smoke at Jay, with a smarmy attitude.

"As I recall, both you and I perused through them together and we both agreed they were trash. We left together, remember?"

"Yes, but you've gone back on several occasions. I know you looked at them again. Sara told me."

"That's true," Jay said with a hint of disgust in his tone. "Can't deny that. Al was in his man cave, and he had to show me a few new magazines. Just had to show me; especially the one of couples who swap partners. I wasn't going to tell him what to

102

do in his own house and Sara wasn't bothered by them. So why should I say anything?" Jay paused. "By the way, I do not like to see women posing and performing in those ways. It's not for me."

"That's hard to believe," Elsa said smugly.

"Then believe this. I don't see Al anymore. He made a suggestion about wife swapping. I nearly clocked him."

"You should have," Elsa said harshly. "He's depraved."

"I know," Jay replied after taking another sip of his coffee. "I wish I would have."

Elsa thought momentarily trying to find a new avenue of contemptuous attack. "You're insolent," were the words that shot out of her mouth.

"And you're history," Jay mumbled softly.

"What was that?"

"I said what does it matter? It's your choice that we sleep in separate rooms. I never wanted that."

"Because you disgust me and snore and fart."

"You think you don't snore or fart when you're sleeping, little lady? Everyone does. Is that why you blow smoke in my face?"

"I don't blow smoke in your face. I don't do those things." She said slowly and evenly with her eyes pinched tightly together.

Jay gave Elsa a hard, piercing glance of his own. "You know," he said after taking sip of his coffee, "there was a time when I felt safe enough to let you into my world because I thought your world was safe. But now I don't know what your problem is. I don't know who you are, or even where you're coming from. I'll tell you this, little girl, I'm damned well getting sick and tired of your degrading remarks and accusations. I don't deserve them. I've tried my best to forgive you and——and love you. But you've been trying real hard to drive——"

Jay suddenly felt dizzy. He dropped his cup, spilling the liquid across the table as he reached out to steady himself with both hands.

"Jay," Elsa shouted; her eyes filled with uncertain opportunity. "What's wrong," she theatrically cried? Hoping he was having a heart attack and then she'd be free to pursue her latest dream.

Jay, wide eyed and trembling, gasped for air as the entire room started spinning out of control and the lights started fading in and out. It's me, he thought. I'm the one to be disposed of. And Elsa knew about this place all along. The signs! She saw the signs and she planned to let me bring her here.

"Jay!" Elsa screamed, trying to break away from him "What's wrong with you? Are you crazy?"

Jay let go of the table and lunged for his wife's neck, his face twisted up with one desire: strangle her before he passed out.

"You won't get away with this. I SWEAR YOU WON'T." Elsa screamed and ducked under the table, dropping her cigarette on the floor. Jay tried to grab his wife's hair and pull her out from under the table. But he failed to make contact. Moreover, it wouldn't have done him any good. The drug was taking control of his body much too fast. He was getting weaker by the second and losing complete control, becoming numb with a darkness settling in. Within seconds he was weak and unable to move. His entire body went limp and his head hit the top of the table. With heavy eyelids, he tried to focus on the beautiful waitress entering the room from the kitchen. But that was impossible. The drug, whatever it was, had done its job and he was losing the battle to stay awake. The last thing he saw before passing out was the lovely waitress blowing him a kiss.

Elsa climbed out from under the table, puzzled but not frightened by Jay's behavior.

"Jay?" She asked softly as she gave him a nudge. "Can you hear me?"

"He can't hear you," Pidge said, sitting next to Jay and lifting his head up to wash off the coffee from his face. "We gave him a sedative."

"A sedative," Elsa asked? "You mean he's still alive? He's not dead?"

"He's sleeping."

"But will he die soon? Maybe tonight?"

"Not tonight," The Waitress said abruptly. She was very displeased by Elsa's questions. She gave Elsa a piercing glance, wanting to reach across the table and slap her silly. She loathed the wicked woman whose only concern was her own gratification and egocentric preoccupations.

"What's going on?"

"Relax, Mrs. Walker," Pidge demanded. "You know what's going on. You activated the ring and knew his curiosity would bring him here when the sign came on. And when he noticed the other signs, he would be so curious he couldn't help but stop."

"Yes, I suppose you're right," Elsa calmly agreed as she looked down at the pinky ring of gold and slowly rotated the band around her finger; trying hard to remember.

"So you do want out of your relationship, don't you," Pidge asked? "But of course you do. Why else would you have stopped here?"

Now it was Elsa's turn to have a lump of fear in her throat. She thought about the road signs Jay had seen on the highway. And then it hit her. Jay wasn't just a little curious about the signs and this place; he had stopped to hopefully dispose of her. "How dare him," she mumbled softly, yet bitterly. "But it had backfired on the creep." She glanced up at the waitress who was fuzzing too much over Jay. "I didn't think he had any hate in him," Elsa said in a bewildered tone. "It was more than curiosity that drove him here. He wondered if he was going to get rid of me tonight. His stupid little act of not really wanting to come here was just a pretense. He was hoping he could kill me, that I'm sure of. The foolish truck driving cheat has been outsmarted. Instead of me, we get rid of him."

"Leave the "we" out of this," The waitress said with disdain in her tone.

"Whatever," Elsa said with a shrug like a valley girl. She chuckled softly and leaned back, smiled, and thought about all the possibilities that were opening up for her. No more Jay to deal with, what a blessing that will be———that is, if this isn't a dream? She sat up and pinched herself, then watched the waitress take care of her soon to be late husband.

"Tell me something," Elsa asked. Her countenance changed to curiosity. "How did you know my name?"

The waitress ignored her question. As far as she was concerned it was a rhetorical query, and she was only trying to make conversation. She despised the wife of this good man she was cleaning; as she looked down at his face she noticed the handsome gentle qualities that anyone who met him could see immediately. She's a fool to want him gone. This rubbed her the wrong way and Pidge had no desire to be in the same room with the wicked witch.

"Pick your cigarette up," Pidge said sharply. "Before it burns a hole in our floor."

Elsa ducked under the table and picked up her cigarette.

"The director will explain everything," Pidge said while Elsa put her cigarette out in the ashtray. "He has the answers to all your questions." Pidge leaned on the table and came face to face with Elsa. "But he will have questions that you must answer truthfully. If you deviate in any way, he'll know, and then you'll be sorry." She pursed her lips together and lowered her voice. "And you'll go without a new husband." She paused to let her threat sink in, and then said in a deep sinister tone: "You may never leave this place. The second time around is not as easy as the first time. I hope you understand what I'm saying?"

Elsa shook her head; clearly she understood what was meant. She realized the waitress must be one of the superiors of this place and that it was best if she listened and obeyed the woman. She also noticed that Jay was right. The waitress did resemble her, and she did sound a tad like her. But that didn't mean a thing right now. She would worry about that later; maybe she would ask the director about the resemblances? But right now she was being offered a new lease on life, a new husband, and a chance to get rid of Jay. She smiled at the thought as two woman dressed in white lab coats wheeled a gurney into the room.

Pidge, while bracing Jay so he wouldn't fall and hit his head on the table again, stood up and helped the two women get the drugged, sleeping Jay out of the booth and place him on the gurney. She helped drape a white sheet over him and then slowly caressed his face and rubbed her left hand through his hair. A warm soothing sensation surged through her as she continued to stroke his hair and she knew that she could love this man with every fiber of her body. She was in love with Jay and when his wife asked her if he was going to die, she turned with an appalled expression on her face that stirred up the deep pain that she had been holding inside of her heart. She was about to say something to put fear into Elsa Walker but the voice of The Director within her mind stopped her. He told her to calm down and she instantly obeyed, knowing he was right and that she would have been out of line. She recalled a part of the oath she had taken when The Director had chosen her to be in charge of the humanoids on his vessel, and had given her power to read minds: *I swear to withhold all my anger and frustrations when dealing with customers.* Using her own ability to telepathically communicate with The Director, she apologized for being tempted, knowing full well the Director was right; it was not her place to be judgmental towards any of the customers, no matter what she thought of them.

"Where are you taking him?" Elsa asked for the fourth time. Again the three waitresses ignored her. She didn't care where or what they did with him, she was merely wondering out loud. They could take him out back and cut him up into a thousand pieces, it just didn't matter. "Do what you want with him," she said. "Just get him out of my life." Then she cheerfully twirled around once and blew him a farewell kiss, extending her arms in his direction like she was sending someone off on the Titanic, never to be seen again.

The three women ignored Elsa's remarks and flippant gestures. The tallest of the two assistants, a striking brunette with dark shoulder length hair and strong brown eyes, removed a manila folder out from under the pillow and gave it to Pidge, then helped push Jay out of the room. Pidge sat back down in the booth and started studying the file while Elsa watched the two women escort Jay out of the room.

"What a relief," she cried, clapping her hands together and smiling. "I can hardly believe he's out of my life." She let out a girlish squeal and pinched herself again. "Thank God this isn't a dream. I think I'd go nuts if I had to put up with him for one more day. You wouldn't believe that man. Did you know he checked the figures on my checkbook every time he came home? I mean every time. It was enough to make me scream. And he did it to make sure I wasn't spending his money on trivial things. It was always his money, you know. It was never our money, just his." Elsa turned to the window and started fussing with her hair, moving back and forth to see all of her reflection in the makeshift mirror. "I think I'll go after a blond. One with strong-arms, a hairy chest and money. He must have money, lots of money. Don't you agree?"

"No," Pidge replied, looking up from the file for the first time and giving Elsa a sardonic face as she noticed that she was living in an imaginary world, vainly admiring herself like the wicked queen saying, mirror, mirror, on the wall—crazy stuff. Pidge wondered what she was flying on. "Money isn't everything."

"Now, that's where you're wrong, girlfriend. In this day and age, you must have money. You're nothing, and I mean nothing, if you don't have it. Believe me, I know." Elsa eyed Pidge for a moment. "Which brings up a point," she said with curiosity edged in her face. "What's this going to cost

115

me? I mean, what do you want for whatever it is you do?"

"The director will discuss that with you. He's the one who determines payment for our services. But there's one thing you should know, Mrs. Walker."

"Call me Elsa."

"We never take money," the waitress went on, ignoring her request. "Never. So calm yourself. This won't cost you a dime. Not one thin dime."

Elsa licked her dry lips and swallowed because her throat suddenly felt tight. "Then what do you take?" She asked, forcing a smile, "Souls?"

Pidge glanced up from the report and gave the nervous woman who was scratching her face and neck like she had an itchy rash, a steady gaze, but remained mysteriously quiet.

Starting out with a slow rub to her forehead then onto an outright scrubbing,

Elsa asked, "What's that," pointing to the file?

"It's a record of your life," Pidge replied, with amused overtones that were obvious in her incredibly strong brilliant green eyes that sparkled like emeralds.

"What do you mean," Elsa asked? She shuddered uncontrollably.

"We've been monitoring your progress since you last used our service." Pidge grinned at the troubled woman; a grin that disturbed Elsa so deeply she felt cold from head to toe.

"Is it cold in here or is it just me," Elsa asked.

"No," Pidge replied. "It's rather hot in here. We keep it at about seventy-two degrees in the winter......Chilly?"

"It must be just me with so much happening right now. Since I last used your service? I——I don't understand?"

"Sure you do. Just think about your dreams. Or should I say _nightmares?_"

Elsa studied the waitress in silence as she thought about her past.

THE NIGHTMARES...(Elsa suddenly grasped the big picture, thinking)...ALL OF THEM WERE TRUE...THEY REALLY DID HAPPEN...THE BRIGHT LIGHTS...THE EERIE NOISES...THE WEIRD SMELLS...HUMANOIDS WALKING THROUGH WALLS...AND THOSE ODD LOOKING CREATURES BENDING OVER HER. EXAMINING HER BY PRODING HER WITH THEIR STRANGE INSTRUMENTS.

"That's right," Pidge said with a closed mouth smile. A smile that sent a cold shiver down Elsa's back for a third time. "Those nightmares that you've discussed with your analyst were real examinations, every last one of them. And "this" is real, too. And the sooner you realize it, and come to your senses, the sooner you can walk out of here," she paused and then in a sinister tone added: "With a new husband."

"You——you're not from here, are you?"

Pidge ignored the question. "There's no need to become agitated," she said. "Everything you need to know will be explained by the director. Be patient."

Elsa stared at the red head for a moment, concealing her fearful thoughts about the waitress. She tried to lock herself behind a veil of feigned courage with other thoughts, including her husband Jay, the man she once loved and was so attracted to because he looked like a Nordic Viking. But who had turned out to be a man of *checks and balances*. "Okay," she said. "Let's get to it. What's the drill? What do I have to do?"

"You'll find out—as soon as the director arrives."

"What's he like?" The waitress ignored Elsa's questions. "Come on, what's he like?"

119

"You'll find out," Pidge replied cordially but equable.

"When," Elsa persisted?

"Soon," Pidge replied firmly. "Just be patient."

Elsa started to respond but remained silent after Pidge gave her a stern look. Woman to woman, Elsa could tell the waitress despised everything about her. But she could care less. She also noticed the way the waitress had touched Jay, caressing his face and rubbing her hand through his hair. As far as she was concerned, if they didn't kill him, the waitress could have him, lock, stock, and barrel; and his lousy trucking job, checking her balances till hell freezes over.

She leaned back in her booth and sighed deeply, then slowly glanced around the room. She was nervous and anxious and her mind was filled with a lot of questions; questions that the waitress, no doubt knew but would not answer. She would have to wait. As she watched the waitress page through the file concerning her life since the last time she had used their service, she tried to recall where and when and how it worked; and why she had chosen Jay for a husband? Surely it wasn't out of love. Was there dating involved? Had she been allowed to date two or three or more men and make up her mind on which she preferred? The more she thought about it, the more her memory seemed to shrink into a thick blanket of fog, complete darkness settling in with no light, no answers coming to mind. How could she be honest if she could not recall the first visit? And the ring—they had given the ring to her, to wear it to keep tabs on her whereabouts. This damn ring was theirs! That's why they had their stupid little file on her. And that meant they knew just when to torture her with those electric jolts in her finger. They know I'm trying to remember things to be honest with them. They're monitoring my thoughts right now—they must be. I need to be honest with the director. If I'm not honest they might give Jay back to me, or someone even more pathetic. Oh, Gawd, she concluded, they know more about me than I do. I must be completely honest; I can't lie to them. I cannot have Jay back in my life, nor can I have another man like him. I'd go mad if that happened.

Elsa was glad she had taken two Valiums earlier. If she had not taken them she knew her anxious thoughts would have her climbing the walls of this—this so-called café.

The director entered the room from the kitchen and crossed the room to the table as though he belonged to a powerful secret society. His dress and demeanor showed that he had the keys of life and death in his hands. He had a dark penetrating stare that saw everything. Was he a just and kind being or one with nothing but contempt for all those who had to sit before him? A strong current of fear surged through Elsa's body like hot lava flowing through her veins. She had seen the tall, well-dressed man before. But he wasn't a man. He was a creature that could change forms. Elsa was sure of it. She was sure of it because she'd seen this——this creature change forms. Elsa tried to recall but only flashes of nightmarish vignettes came and went faster and faster as the Director came closer and closer.

The director gave Pidge a subtle nod as she moved out of the booth, and then he sat across from Elsa. He cupped his well-manicured, manly right hand over the end of his perfectly formed nose that had a thick black mustache under it, setting his elbow on the table and grinned so long with those dark intense eyes that it made her feel like she was having an orgasm. Wow! She thought: he looks just like Tom Selleck this time. He asked her how she felt with undisguised pleasure on his face.

Elsa felt embarrassed. "Okay," she heard herself say in a low voice. They locked eyes for what seemed an eternity. The Director broke the silence.

"So, we meet again," he said in his deep baritone voice. Elsa slowly nodded but remained silent. "Don't concern you with me," he said. "The future is what you need to seriously consider. Is that acknowledged?" Elsa found herself locked in his dark, mirror-like eyes that she could see herself in; eyes that were hypnotic and unearthly cold. There seemed to be a film over each eye that interchanged from a reptilian horizontal black slit, into a dark, round pupil. She nodded in subservient silence. The director leaned slightly forward. "You've been a naughty one since our last visit together. (He didn't respect her enough to call her a woman. She felt diminished by his statement), getting married to Jay—the man that you picked. And then, you forget all about us. You didn't even send us a card as instructed, or write us a thank you letter, again, as instructed; especially if you moved. That was the "wrong" thing to do Mrs. Walker. Don't you agree?" Elsa nodded and swallowed so hard that it sounded like a gulp and she was unable to remove her eyes from his pulsating orbs. He had her in a controllable trance and was reading her thoughts, harvesting her thoughts in a knit-picking action. Revelations of her past began to flash quickly in her thoughts.

"Relax," The Director said evenly. "You're trying to hard; your mind is racing with a lot of uncertainties surfacing; reflective moments I don't need to consider." He reached over and took her right hand in his to help ease her troubled soul. "Nevertheless, I'm not surprised to see that you're extremely troubled concerning your life since our last visit. You feel it's been an extremely hard life. But then again that's only due to your own entitled selfishness." He picked up her file, paged through it rather quickly and then dropped it on the table. "People who are, shall we say, arrogant, self-serving, and entitled, have no meaningful concern for others. I find that rather upsetting and detestable." Elsa slowly nodded her head up and down.

The Director leaned back and expressed his displeasure with a long drawn-out sigh. He placed his right hand on the table and started drumming his fingers. "I must say that out of all the planets within this galaxy that I have been assigned, this one is my favorite. It's such a beautiful sphere and you have so many, many wonderful sights to enjoy; colorful mountains and valleys; so many varieties of plants, flowers, and trees. Wonderful and awesome varieties of wildlife; and of course, so many talented artists: painters, musicians, and especially writers. I love to read the books that all the humanoids that live here have created. They're so fascinating and enlightening. I've learned much about this beautiful world of yours, through this planet's writers. Are you a reader Mrs. Walker?"

Elsa shook her head from side-to-side. "Not like—"

The Director raised his right hand and she stopped in midsentence. "I've read this nation's constitution, several times, and quite a few things about it puzzle me. I've also read articles explaining the purpose of the Preamble as to why it was written. To make it short and sweet, it was a letter to the world justifying why Americans had to secede from England and to state that they could govern themselves by forming a republic and legislate their own set of laws by instituting their own form of government. The biggest mystery that I see, and it has a lot to do with my interacting with people such as you, is in the declarative remark: '*and in the pursuit of happiness.*'" The Director stopped drumming his fingers. He shifted a bit and leaned in toward Elsa. "That's everyone's problem," he said in a more direct tone. "No one that has sat before me has ever really felt content. In fact, those who have sat where you are sitting have all felt extremely hopeless. And because of their misery, their lack of happiness, some have chosen to use drugs to discover their exuberance—more cheerful— only to be disappointed—extremely disillusioned. Others have chosen dead end habitual habits, alcohol, sex, or all three. I myself have tried a couple of your concoctions: wines, beers, but found them all to be rather overrated. Anything when not used as properly intended is a mistake; it breaks my heart. Nonetheless, no one who has indulged themselves in pills, narcotics, sex, or alcohol has escaped from their consequences, or successfully found the happiness that's mentioned in your constitution." He paused momentarily. "That's your problem Mrs. Walker. You are not, as the saying goes, a happy camper." He smiled, trying to make a point. When he saw it had gone over her head, he continued with his dissertation: "You are a miserable, depressed woman who has sought out all the wrong things; for all the wrong reasons. In any universe you live in, that just doesn't work. You also tried to find joy and peace through friends, and male companions. Psychiatrists, astrologers and shopping sprees; shall I go on? RIGHT! And those did-not-work either. In short, your pursuits have all fallen flat on wasted time and energy. You want it all without putting any effort into what others can do for you; you believe you're entitled. But you are not entitled. Nor can you find happiness through others. It must form within your own heart and soul." The Director paused to allow Elsa to consider his critique of her. Elsa was speechless. She just sat there looking at The Director without anything to say. The Director continued: "You are searching without wanting to accept any blame or consequence for your choices; which brings us back to the here and now. We tried to help you when you first came into our establishment south of here. But you, a selfish person in search of your own pleasures; just never once tried hard enough to make it work. So, here we are again."

"It wasn't just me," Elsa said. "You have to—"

"I suppose I should inform you of a few things," he said, holding up his hand and cutting her off. "Just so you completely understand. We must sign an updated agreement before you receive your new husband. A husband that will provide you with all the things you feel you're entitled to, that will fill all your hearts desires. Yes, we know all about your desires and dreams. But I seriously doubt they'll ever make you happy." He paused and nodded his head from side-to-side. Raising his thick black eyebrows, and kissing the tips of his fingers like a mafia Don, then bringing his broad shoulders up along both sides of his head, he said in a musical tone, "They're not at all like the ones you had your choice of, when you first used our services. He gave Elsa a smile that sent a cold shiver up and down her back again. "This time around your choices will be slightly different. But first, you must agree to give us something in return." He leaned back, releasing the spell he had over her.

"What do you want?" Elsa asked. Her eyes were sore and red from having them left open within the trance. She rubbed at them to remove some of the tears that had almost immediately begun to form—to sooth her pupils.

"Something that you, yourself, do not wish to have," he replied hungrily, his mouth appearing to drool. "You failed to deliver on

131

your first promise after you walked out of our little concern north of Moscow, Idaho. So now your payment must be your first two children, to provide us with a delicious _Thyestean banquet_."

"I——ee, don't understand!"

"I'm not surprised," the director said with a self-evident attitude. "Most selfish people refuse to see the fair scope of things. Humans see and hear everything but some claim the right to select only the parts of reality that will benefit them, and what they want to admit. Everything else is conveniently swept under the rug." He clicked his tongue to declare victory over his last rhetorical statement. The director leaned in closer, and as Elsa breathed in, she could taste his warm, reptilian breath. "But I shall help you to fully understand the way of things, Mrs. Walker. You do want to understand all of this, don't you?"

"Yes," Elsa replied slowly, dishonestly nodding her head.

The director smiled. He knew she was being dishonest, he could feel it flowing in every part of her body; in fact, he could even smell it.

"Good," he said. "The first thing you need to know is that, "I" am an Alien. An alien who considers, hmm, how can I say this delicately?" He rubbed his clasped hands hungrily together that sounded like the slithering of a snake. "Human flesh is a delicacy for us," he said with a gleeful reddish twinkle in his eyes. He flicked his tongue out of his mouth and a bit of spray of the transparent green saliva spattered on Elsa face, "especially young flesh." The director paused to let that information register in Elsa's mind. Her eyes and mouth opened slowly at the same time, feeling dry. She was thunder struck, traumatized and felt roiling and gurgling in her bowels, and then felt sick to her stomach. "Oh, please spare me the drama Mrs. Walker. Surely this news can't be that bad for you to digest? Not for a woman who had an abortion prior to her eighteenth birthday. And another abortion shortly before you married the man we provided for you. So I suggest you stop tormenting yourself and think about what you must do. In the past, you have unwittingly given us your fertile eggs. Eggs that were, shall we say, harvested and processed for consumption—with love."

"Processed? With love?" Elsa heard herself say? She felt as if she were being swallowed up in a dark, eternal nightmare with no way out. "You make it sound as though they were raised, well fed, taken care of, and then butchered in a slaughter house."

"That's one way of looking at it," The Director said, agreeably. "In fact, that is precisely what happened to your eggs. But unlike your procedures, we waste nothing. Everything, and I mean everything, is consumed."

"Everything," Elsa asked?

134

"That's right," The Director said. "We even harvest your genes and make specialized growth elixirs out of them—as well as aphrodisiacs and cosmetics from these little yearlings' afterbirth. Isn't that how your own abortionists use the children they harvest?" The Director did not wait for her to answer as the question was rhetorical. "We are much more caring of the mother's health. You see, we take the eggs and grow them into yearlings, or we allow the natural mother to carry her child to full term. It all hinges on the circumstance—the mother's condition. I don't know all the scientific logic behind it, so I never truly delve into the reasons our staff decides on this procedure or another. Are you with me?"

Elsa remained reticent, not knowing what to say.

"If you were a connoisseur of veal," he said after a brief pause, "you would come to understand that we are no different than

135

humans. Our choice of meat isn't that far off from yours. We consider humans the same way you consider young calves. And on my planet, there's a tremendous appetite for young, healthy humanoids. Or should I say veal or yearlings?" The Director chuckled at Elsa's discomfort. He was enjoying himself at her expense. "We, too, call them yearlings," he went on. "Just like your cattle, humans are a part of *our* food chain. Well, not all of you are. The ones who are considered to be in "*THE NEW RACE*" are off limits."

"The new race?"

"The people of *The Book*."

"The Book?"

"That's what I said, *The Book*. But the rest of you who have no ethics or moral background can be picked out and taken to my planet, placed in one of our colonies, observed for a few days, placed where needed and eventually processed for consumption—whether you want to believe it or not."

"But it's not the same. I mean we have the ability to think. To care and have compassion and we——"

"Have a soul," The Director finished her thought. "Only those who join the new race truly believe that. In fact, according to *The Book* there are three classifications of your kind: Natural, Carnal, and Spiritual. The Spiritual ones are the untouchables. Those are well documented and broken down as immortals. As for the others, it's of no concern to us if you are a natural or a feral carnal type. We have no problems identifying and selecting the ones we can take—that is, out of those two groupings."

"How do you see me?" Elsa asked, almost in a whisper.

"You're a natural humanoid."

"Then must I give you a child, my first born?"

"No. Your first child and your second child must be turned over to us. You failed to give us one after we gave you your precious Jay. So we shall require two this time around. That shall be the price for your new husband. And me, well I receive a better price for yearlings that have gone full term within a woman's womb of your age. You see, I——"

The Director suddenly became silent. His face turned cold and his eyes transformed into burning embers. He grabbed the edge of the table with both hands and squeezed until his fingers were pale and ashen. Elsa tried to turn away from the director's piercing eyes but couldn't. She was caught up in his trance again.

"Now I understand," The Director said in a deep hissing tone, with his eyes turning a deep dark shade of red, "you no longer have the ability to have children or produce fertile eggs," he said venomously. He studied Elsa for what seemed like an

138

eternity to her. "You had your female organs removed. You were blocking that information from me. I knew there was something wrong. I knew you were hiding something. And now I know precisely what it is."

"I had a partial hysterectomy," Elsa confessed, her voice trembling with fear.

"Which means you also lied to your husband for quite some time," Elsa started to answer but the director cut her off. "This changes things Mrs. Walker. You must be altered."

"Altered?"

"You and I will be trading places," Pidge informed the woman.

"Please!" Elsa shouted. Her face became terrified and twisted with pain. "You can't do this!" She protested; her entire body quivering.

"It's too late," The Director said coldly. He looked at the young waitress for a brief moment and she quickly left the room. "Your actions have been selfish," The Director said after turning to face the terrified woman. "You have been thoughtlessly and heartlessly dishonest with a man who, at one time, would have done most anything for you."

The director closed his eyes for a moment. Elsa could see his eyes twirling around and around behind his eyelids at a fast pace. This went on for a good thirty seconds as he searched through all the areas of his brain mass for information. The silence was deafening and Elsa could hear her ears ringing and her heart pounding wildly against her chest. And from the corner of her eyes, she could see the cold wind blowing through the trees and shaking the large windows. "Please," Elsa said, her voice shaking as bad as the rest of her body. "I'll do—"

The Director in black opened his eyes and with one look into Elsa's fearful eyes, she stopped begging. He heard the Director inside her mind tell her that begging wouldn't do her any good.

"I'm afraid that you must be taken downstairs," The Director said coldly, his eyes fixated on Elsa's, "to drain all your thoughts and memories of the life you have ever known." Elsa let out a long and anguished cry. "And, if you are lucky, given a second chance——that is, if we can replace your uterus and ovaries and give you the gene therapy to cleanse your body from excess natal hormones to prevent cancer. But if not, well it will be an unpleasant ending." The director licked his thin, cold lips and eyed Elsa intently. That drove her over the edge. She began to weep and tremble uncontrollably. Pidge and the same two lab assistants that took Jay into the back came in and, after giving her a shot in the arm and securing her to the gurney, removed her from the room. The director and Pidge remained silent as they listened to Elsa being delivered to the processing room. When the second and final door had been closed with a metallic thud, Pidge sat across from the director and smiled.

"I know that smile," he said. "You want to go with this Jay, don't you?"

"It is my time, is it not?"

"Yes, it's your time. But are you sure you will be happy with this man?"

"I like him. In fact I was deeply saddened to see him go off with that woman when she chose him. I'd been visiting with him and he was so interesting. I was pleased to see him return. I want to try."

"Why?"

"Intuition," Pidge responded. "My humanistic traits are telling me he's the one for me."

"Are you sure you want to be a part of this——barbaric society, with all its ethnic, social, and economic troubles? Not to mention how far behind they are in the sciences on this beautiful planet they call Earth."

"I'm sure. I want to have children. And I know that Jay and I can provide your people with a healthy——"

"That won't be necessary," The Director said, raising his hand to cut her off. "You have served us well. And the eggs we have extracted from you have all been fertile. There will be no need for us to take your first born. You have my word on that."

"Thank you for all you have done for me." Her voice was full of joy.

The director smiled. "Go! Have them give you all of her history. I will talk with this man while you prepare yourself."

Pidge smiled at the Director and thanked him again. She gave him a quick kiss on the forehead and vanished behind the double doors just as the two lab assistants ushered Jay into the room and carefully placed him back in the booth.

As soon as they were alone, the Director reached over and placed a hand on Jay's head. He stirred briefly and then slowly opened his eyes. He sat back in the booth and stared at the Director in wonder.

"What's going on," He asked? His voice cracked a bit in his drowsiness. He looked around and asked: "I thought I was sitting where you're sitting?"

"You were."

"Who are you?"

"Who I am doesn't matter. Just call me a friend."

Jay studied him in silence for a moment and then asked: "Where's my wife?"

"She'll be back shortly."

"Is she okay?"

"Yes, she's fine," The Director replied.

"You the owner?"

"You could say that."

Jay looked around the room. "What can I do for you?"

"Answer a few questions."

144

"What kind of questions?"

"Questions that concern you."

"Me," Jay replied, feeling confused, "Why?"

"To satisfy my curiosity," The Director replied. "I am extremely curious about and what you do."

"I've done quite a few things in my life," Jay replied. "But right now I drive long haul. I'm a truck driver."

"Yes, that's what your wife has told us. Tell me, I understand truck drivers are a special breed of people. They have wanderlust in their hearts and in their souls. Do you find that to be true?"

"I suppose." Jay rubbed his eyes and yawned. "If you don't have it, you don't make it in the business. It's not for the ones who like to go home every night, or work forty hour weeks and have weekends off, that's for sure."

145

"Tell me, are you one of those drivers who must have a woman at various places when you stop?"

Jay leaned back against the booth and studied the man in black for a few seconds, noticing that he looked a lot like Tom Selleck, and thought the man's eyes were inquisitive, yet cold, and somewhat dangerous. They were also eyes that slightly warned him to be honest; eyes that seemed to undulate and that was now putting him in a deep trance, a deep trance that was allowing this odd sort of fellow to enter into his mind, to feed him information and to read his thoughts. Jay tried to blink and to turn his head to the side, but the trance was too powerful. The only thing he could do was to just sit and stare back at the man's examining eyes.

"You can be verbal, Jay," The Director said, releasing him from the trance. "Please, answer my question."

146

"No," Jay said slowly, wishing he could wash down the dryness in his throat with a glass of water. "I don't do that. Some do and some just say they do. To make themselves look good."

"Why?"

"I don't know," Jay replied with a shrug. "There are a lot of braggarts out there."

"And you've never considered it?"

"Couple of times, perhaps? But I never pursued it."

The director smiled and leaned forward, placing his arms on the table.

"Why did you stop here at this establishment? What were you hoping to find?"

Jay hesitated.

"Come now, Jay. You know why and I know why, right?"

"Yes," he replied slowly, shaking his head up and down. "I saw signs alongside

147

the highway. Signs that said something about a spouse disposal site. I thought that was odd and my curiosity got the best of me."

"The signs were not for you to see."

"They were for my wife?"

"That's right." The Director paused to read Jay's thoughts. "And since you were having a troubled time with your wife, you thought if we did what the signs said, you could dispose of your wife."

"I thought about it. But I wasn't really sure if I could go through with it."

"Yes, I know. I've been studying you. You're actually a good man. That's good to know."

"I thought it was a prank at first. But then I saw two more signs." Jay leaned his own arms on the table and was almost face to face with the Director. "To be honest," he said, almost whispering, "I was hoping to find out more about this place. That is——if it's truly a place where one can get rid of or

148

exchange their spouse. Is that what this place is, a Spouse Disposal Site?"

"Do you love your wife?" The Director asked, ignoring Jay's queries.

"I did. But she drove my love away with her lies and her cheating."

"You know about her cheating, huh?"

"Yes. She's even having an affair with my ex-boss."

"How do you know this?"

"You just told me. You're putting the truth about Elsa inside my head."

"Am I?"

"Yes. You just told me you were."

"Do you believe me?"

"Yes."

"What am I telling you now?"

"That you have arranged for me to have a loving and caring wife and that if I ever hurt her, you will be back to straighten me out. And that your scientists have developed an aphrodisiac made from the genes and pheromones of both male and female humans."

"Do you believe that I can do that?"

"Yes."

"Who am I Jay?"

"You're The Director."

"Of what?"

"Many things," Jay said slowly.

"You're an astute young man. And, from reading your mind, I can see that you can be a loving husband and father. But you also harbor a lot of aversion for your wife. You must rid your thoughts and your memory of those feelings to be a successful husband. When I snap my fingers you will go back to sleep and when you awake, you will recall nothing of this meeting and you will have nothing but the highest respect and love for your wife. Do you understand?"

"Yes. I understand."

"Here are two vials of special vitality serum for you and your wife. I want you to take them when you feel lonely or tempted to stray." The Director smiled and snapped his fingers. In an instant Jay fell forward, his head coming to rest on his arms. The Director stood, moved to the window and observed the cold and windy night, waiting for Pidge to return and claim her husband. She didn't keep him waiting long. As she entered the room through the swinging doors just beyond the counter, the Director watched the cold wind blow a long stream of snow across the frozen parking lot, under the semi, over a small mound of snow, and into the trees just beyond the parking lot. He also caught the trees swaying gently as the wind caught their limbs and branches. Most of the clouds were now gone and the full blue moon shone brightly through the trees, making it a lovely winter's night.

"I love winter," The Director said, without turning to look at the lovely woman. "It's my favorite time of the year to visit this planet." He slowly turned and smiled at

Pidge, now dressed in Elsa's clothes. "What's your favorite season, my dear?"

"I like them all," she said, returning his smile.

"Then you shall have no problem adjusting to this world again," he said, taking her by her right arm and escorting her back to the booth and sitting her down directly across from Jay.

"Remember," The Director said, "once you've placed your hands on his you will not remember a thing about us." A couple of other things you need to know, I gave Jay two vials of genetic hormone therapy with your pheromones in one and jays pheromones in the other. You take the blue vial and Jay must take the brown one. You will always be attracted to only each other. There are sixty drops in each vial. You and Jay take one drop every year from your own."

"Thank you," Pidge said warmly.

The Director smiled and thanked her again for all her help, and then added: "Jay is close to becoming a person of "The Book" an immortal, an untouchable." The Director paused. "Well, not quite an immortal. He's still a carnal man, but he's trying to become spiritual. That makes him and you off limits to any of our other agents. I doubt if you will have any issues with us. Besides, you have a ring and you will know what to do if something does come up."

"I understand."

"Now, as soon as you hold his hands, you will know his complete history and all the negative feelings that Elsa gave him will be gone. You will have nothing to worry about."

"What about him?" She asked, nodding toward Jay.

The Director smiled. "He's a good man. He will love you like you've never been loved before. Within the home that you'll

153

share with Jay, he will place you and keep you within the place of honor." The Director paused to hold Pidge in his eyes. "But stay away from Me-isms. They destroy relationships. Once you have slipped into a Me-ism, it's hard to break out of it. Everything for me: me this, me that; me, me, me first——and you will lose this man."

"I know," Pidge said. "I saw it in her eyes. His wife thought only of herself. She was a dreadful person. I will not do that."

"I do believe you'll always know love," The Director said with a warm hearted feeling. "I believe that I shall miss you dearly."

Pidge looked up at the director and smiled. The Director returned her smile. He kissed her forehead and then left the room, careful not to touch the white counter or the swinging doors that led into the disposal site's dark and mysterious vaults. Pidge sat across from Jay and placed his hands in hers and squeezed them tight, feeling the warm

154

essence of his love surging through her body and the burning desire of wanting to have a child move and grow in her womb. She also allowed his memory banks to fill hers with his entire life; the process took about two minutes to complete. When it was over she knew Jay was the right man for her.

Jay opened his eyes and smiled across the table at Pidge. He felt invigorated, alive, and in love with his wife.

"Let's go home," she said warmly, squeezing his hands again. "My father can wait."

"Are you sure?" Jay asked, feeling his heart racing a little faster. "I——I really don't mind go——"

"You were right about him. He just pretends to be sick. So let's just go home, take the phone off the hook, and cuddle the way we used to."

Jay leaned over the table and gave Pidge a kiss. "You know," he said in a romantic tone, "we can make love in the truck. Something I've always wanted to do. The load doesn't deliver until ten-thirty in the morning. We've come this far so let's just stay the night here, huh?"

"Okay," Pidge replied softly. "I can handle that."

"You sure?"

"Yes, I'm sure," Pidge replied. "We can spend the night here."

Jay climbed out of the booth and helped Pidge with her coat. He checked the time on his wristwatch, thought about saying something, but played it off with a shrug. A good forty-five plus minutes had passed since he had entered the diner—yet he could not remember a thing about the visit. He shrugged his shoulders again, tossed a few dollars on the table, and with Pidge by his side, stepped into the cold winter's night. They almost slipped on the ice a few times but managed to stay afoot, laughing and holding on to each other tightly.

The Director, sitting in the darkness of his office above the restaurant, watched the two lovers leave the café and walk across the parking lot and enter the truck. He sighed deeply, wondering why he felt so sad about her leaving; after all, he had others to fill the void. For over seventy-five Earth years he had come to this planet to help abused women and the abducted runaways and troubled youths, and collect sperm donors for their colonies back home without so much as one thought about their feelings——that is, until he had saved Pidge from the hands of her painful and lonely life-style.

And he had grown rather found of her, letting her serve on the ship instead of being placed in one of the colonies back home, to do nothing but produce eggs and then be devoured herself. She had been a good servant, doing what was needed without complaint. Through his studies of this world's ways, he knew he loved the young woman—that is, in his own way—but he also knew he could never do anything about it. He was extremely proud of the way she had worked out and the way their friendship had bloomed. He was happy to see her finally in love with a good man.

He was going to miss her deeply, but it had been her choice to leave, to have children, to be a part of the human race again, to experience the joys of love and the pain and suffering of this barbaric planet. He had made a promise to her and she had decided to go back and love a man that would treat her right. At least she would not remember the bad things of her life before he had found her, and that was good.

A knock on his door brought him out of his thoughts.

"Come," he said loudly without turning around.

"We have a message." The lab assistant with the stunning figure and dark hair said after entering the room. "It's from

158

operations." She moved to the desk. "The message is as you expected. Make no contact with any of the people who run the abortion clinics. It was a unanimous decision. They want you to continue your operation per standing operation procedures."

"I see," The Director said thoughtfully. "I suppose they are waiting for a few more teams to arrive from Alton to open our own clinics. That makes sense. We do have over thirty now throughout America alone."

"The message states that fifty-two new humanoid graduates are on their way to us now. Their arrival should be within a few days."

"Go on. Give me the rest of the message," The Director said softly, as he continued to watch the snow snake its way across the parking lot and under the trailer of the big rig.

"It concerns," The lovely woman stopped to clear her throat.

The Director turned and eyed the woman, reading her thoughts. "Yes, it is such a waste, my dear. A terrible waste of flesh; all those babies, hundreds of them on a daily basis being butchered and discarded like unwanted toys--while making only minuscule advances in what they refer to as science. I am pleased that you feel the way you do."

"I just don't understand the committee's decision? Your species has all the technology to carry the aborted babies to full term and———and———"

"Thank you for being so concerned. But you must not let it get you down. I will submit another proposal with additional facts and perhaps some photos after the new interns arrive. Now, tell me the rest of the message."

"But you already know what it is. You've been reading my thoughts."

"Yes, but I like the sound of your voice. So, humor me. Speak."

"The committee feels that the operative in Pittsburgh has been dishonest and careless about his activities. In fact, he has been compromised and they want him brought in. There have been far too many unsolved murders and they strongly believe he's involved. They want him picked up before the police get him."

"Go on," The Director said evenly.

"If——if it is true and you bring him in, I would like to be the one to inform him of his fate. After all, you saved me from him and I have——"

"Don't worry," The Director said with a wave of his hand. "You shall have the pleasure. I, like you, have been waiting for this day. I have never liked that repulsive man."

Lola smiled. Her smile pleased the Director.

161

"Thank you," she said. "I've waited a long time for this moment. But why did the committee allow this man to operate?"

"We don't focus or ask any questions concerning their decisions. We only press forward and when a few are replaced we can make suggestions."

"I understand. I am just curious."

"There are far too many other procedures and answers you must concern yourself with—now that Pidge is gone. Be patient and keep your eyes and ears open. But do not question anyone higher than me. You could find yourself in serious trouble that even I could not get you out of." The Director paused momentarily. "As to the question you are now thinking, don't ask it. But I will tell you this. The committee allowed a few operatives to continue abducting because, to put it mildly, they are blind to our ways. They have no idea who we are, or what we do with their victims. They love the money we give them for their abductees." A moment of silence filled the room as the two exchanged glances. "So tell me," The Director asked, "how do you feel about returning to your home planet? You're next in line, you know?"

"I have no desire to come back to this dreadful place. It's too cruel and too deadly; too much fear lingers in far too many places." She moved to the window and looked at the cold night for a few moments. She turned to face the Director. "I like it here and I like my job. It gives me a sense of belonging. One I've never known before."

"Then you shall stay as long as you wish."

"Thank you."

The Director stood and walked around the table and stood in front of her. "I am going to give you control of the others. You shall be given more power." He placed his hands over her ears. "Don't be afraid. You will feel a small electrical charge, but it will

163

not harm you." The Director inserted his thumbs in each of her ears. "Relax and close your eyes. Be not afraid."

Lola did as she was told. Shortly, she felt a tingle move from right to left through her brain, causing her to shudder a little during the procedure. It lasted a good fifteen to twenty seconds. The Director removed his hands from her ears. Her body felt numb but she was able to stand erect.

"How do you feel," he asked?

"A bit dizzy and excited," she replied, "And at peace."

"Good. It worked. Now reach out with your thoughts and tell me what you see and hear."

Lola looked up at The Director.

"Keep your eyes closed," he said, almost in a whisper. His voice was soft and soothing. "Reach out with all your senses. Tell me what you see and hear."

164

Lola closed her eyes and began the task as instructed. Within a minute she smiled; this told the Director that she was in contact.

"What do you see and hear," he asked.

"I see the man and Pidge in the truck down in the parking lot. There is so much peace, so much joy, and they're laughing and holding each other in an embrace."

"Good," The Director said. "Now come back into this room. Look into my eyes and read them. If you can see what is in my eyes, you will fully understand the reasons I did not allow you or the others to leave this ship when we returned to Alton."

Lola did as instructed. She moved a few steps closer and looked up into the unblinking eyes of her boss. It didn't take her long to discover the truth.

"Oh no," She exclaimed, placing her right hand over her mouth. "The committee! All of them! They wanted to devour us. But you wouldn't let them. You had and have the

165

power to stop anyone from coming onto your ship and taking us from you. You saved our lives." She stepped back a few steps. "Thank you, Sir. I know I can serve you well."

"I know you can. And I know you will," The Director said with a warm smile. He walked around to the back of his desk and opened the top right drawer. He pulled out a beautiful necklace of gold with a heart shaped pendant that had a sparkling bright red ruby set with small diamonds around it. He came back around the desk and motioned Lola to turn around. He slipped the chain around her neck.

"This is and will always be your protection and your power source. It will help you to do what is right at all times. Never take it off, not even when you sleep. And don't worry about anyone else trying to remove it. They will be severely punished for trying, or even thinking about it. You and I are the only ones who can remove it. But my recommendation to you now is to wear it at all times."

"It's so lovely."

"You deserve it, my dear. It is just as powerful as the one I gave Pidge when I promoted her. But this one is slightly different in color. Again, the one place you never want to remove it from your neck is when we are back on Alton. You will be at the mercy of greedy, hungry fools who love to devour women from this planet."

"Thank you. I'll never take it off."

"You have been given a special gift. The highest I can give to any of my servants. When others see the necklace they will know you are second in command and powerful. They'll also know that you will grow in power and be able to read their minds." The Director leaned back on his desk and let his countenance turn serious. "But there is a curse that comes with this new power. Listen to me now. I picked you out of all the others because of your loyalty and because you have no hardcore hatred, no envy, and no jealousy or bitterness in your heart. Oh, the man in Pittsburgh deserves your scorn and you can toy with him in any way you desire. But I know, despite all that he's done to you, you have not been tempted to destroy or hurt the others we have transported back to Alton— or kept on this ship for artificial insemination. It's not in your nature to be spiteful. You must always keep yourself calm, compassionate, and above all else, show mercy and fairness to everyone you judge to be worthy. Is that clear?"

"Yes," Lola replied, holding back her tears. "But what's the curse?"

"If you lose one or more of your attributes that I have mentioned, or if you become much too judgmental, you will become mean spirited and almost demonic. Your eyes will become dark and sinister, your nose will grow long, your hair will become a dull grey, wiry and unkempt, and

168

your entire body will wrinkle up like a wad of paper. You will lose your status and become an outcast; none, not even the humanoids of this planet, will help you. In essence, you will experience a cruel, lonely death."

Lola looked down at the necklace and toyed with it in her fingers. Shortly, she looked at the Director. "I won't let that happen. I promise."

The Director smiled. "Good girl. Now, let's go to work."

Lola smiled. "Okay."

The Director took her by the arm and walked her to the door. "How does it look for our new passenger?"

"We found a match. Her ovaries and uterus can be replaced."

"Good," The Director said with raised eyebrows as he opened the door. After closing the office door, he smiled down at Lola. "Have the procedure done before we leave."

"And when will that be?"

"Within a week," The Director replied. "We need a few more sperm donors before we go. But it won't be long, I assure you."

"I love space travel."

"Where is our new passenger, in the outer room?"

"Yes. Do you wish to speak with her?"

"I do."

Together they walked down a small hallway to a door on the left. They entered and observed Elsa on the gurney she had been placed on in the restaurant. Her clothes had all been removed and she was now covered with a white sheet. The room was clean and an antiseptic aroma strongly permeated throughout the cubicle that resembled an operating room. The Director approached the table and snapped his fingers. Elsa opened her blurry eyes.

"Before we put you under again," The Director said with a tight-lipped grin, "there are a few facts that you should know. And if

170

you have any brains, you may have already figured some of them out, now haven't you?"

Elsa slowly nodded her head up and down.

"Did you finally comprehend that you have traded places with your twin sister?" Again, Elsa nodded. "A sister that you had no idea existed?" Again, Elsa nodded her head. Tears began to run from the corner of her eyes.

The Director picked up Elsa's left hand. "I almost forgot the ring. Let's take it off your finger." Elsa started to tell him it wouldn't come off, but he told her to stop talking with his dark sinister looking eyes. He wrapped his left hand around her little finger and slowly removed the ring without any pain to Elsa. "Ah, that wasn't so bad, now was it?"

Elsa looked at the small ring the Director held up in front of her. More tears and make up streamed down the sides of her face; the nurse standing next to her wiped off the dark lines of makeup from her face with a white sterile cloth.

"I see some marks on the ring," The Director said as he examined the band. "You were trying to have it removed." He shook his head from side-to-side while clicking his tongue. "We told you to never try to have it removed. That it was yours and only yours." He looked down at Elsa's little finger. "I see the ring punished you. How could you be so foolish as to think you could remove this ring when you were told you must never do it?" Elsa remained motionless. She was petrified and found it hard to answer his question. The nurse wiped hot tears from her face again, but a little harder. The Director gave Lola the ring. "You are going to be watched closely during your stay. Don't do anything more to get into trouble. Now, would you care to know what happened? Just why you are here with us now?"

172

Elsa nodded and blinked her eyes a few times. "Yes, I would," she managed to say in a raspy whisper.

"As you know, your mother died while giving birth to you and your sister. Your father, who truly loved your mother, was overcome with grief; so much grief that he could not bear to look at the two of you; so he turned you and your sister over to your aunt, who was, to say the least, quite troubled herself. She took you on for money, lots of money. But within a few months, she decided that it wasn't enough. She found it difficult to meet the demands of motherhood. She wanted more money from your father but he refused. So, your aunt sold your sister to a friend, a friend who moved out of state, a friend who had a husband with a drinking problem and, when your sister became a teenager, he started molesting her. She ran away and we picked her up off the streets of Seattle a few years later. She produced eggs for us and, when I lost one of my servants, I took her under my charge. She was an excellent worker and she became a dear friend. But she always longed to come back to this barbaric planet, to full-fill the need to be loved and to love. Unlike you, she wanted children, lots of children. She yearned for motherhood. So, when you and Jay came along, we made the switch."

Elsa shook her head from side-to-side with hot tears running down her face.

"I——'m so sorry," she said pitifully. "Please forgive me, I beg you. Please!"

"Oh, but we have. And we shall be using you for egg production. You see, we have found a match and you will have new female organs replaced inside of your body."

Elsa's demeanor changed with the news. "I think I'd just as soon die," Elsa hissed, as she glared up at the Director with hatred while trying to remove the straps to jump off the table. "You're all a bunch of sick freaks. How can you do that, give me a uterus? I hate you." She kept on struggling. The Director and nurses stepped back to watch her for a few minutes. They approached the table when she finally gave up.

"Calm yourself," The Director said in his authoritarian voice. "It won't do you any good to go on like a mad woman. We are much too busy to listen to your temper tantrums."

"You monster, you evil piece of Alien garbage. Let me out of here," Elsa demanded.

"Everything that will be happening to you from here on out was brought on by your own lies and deceit. We gave you what you wanted when you first used our services. Jay was a wonderful and loving husband to you. We could not and would not replace him with one of those so-called blond hunks with money you so greedily wanted. You deceived us from the start and that cannot and will not be overlooked. You're here to stay so get used to it and behave yourself. And don't give it one bit of concern about the number of babies that you will produce for us. It has no bearing on how we treat you humanoids."

The Director looked over at Lola. "She'll be your first charge. Treat her kindly but strictly."

"I will do as you say," Lola replied.

He turned towards the door, but then looked over his shoulder at Lola. "You can take over, my dear. She's all yours."

Lola thanked the director and then moved to Elsa's bedside. She was sobbing quietly but the look in her eyes told Lola she wanted to choke the life out of her. Lola looked at her with a sense of peace and compassion in her eyes. She had no bitterness or hatred for Elsa.

"If you do well while on board this ship, you will soon come to understand that no one here will harm you. But you must first undergo a period of developing fetuses and nursing them. How long, I can't say. Please do yourself a favor and behave yourself. The Director is sincere and will give you a position of trust someday. That is, if you have a change of attitude and become part of the team. It will depend entirely on you. Is that clear?"

Elsa was filled with rage, yet listened quietly to Lola who was in charge. She wanted to scream; the thought of being used to produce babies outraged her.

"Trust me," Lola said softly after leaning into Elsa's outraged countenance. "You don't want to be taken off this ship and placed in one of the colonies back on Alton."

"Colony," Elsa asked with a blank look in her troubled eyes.

"You wouldn't last long in one of them," Lola said. "There you are issued a number and when it comes up, you will be processed for consumption." She smiled at Elsa and stood erect. "So from here on out just do as you're told."

"Must I have sex," Elsa asked in a quivering voice?

"No," Lola replied. "You will always be artificially inseminated." Lola gave her a warm smile and then snapped her fingers. Elsa quickly sunk into a deep sleep before she could scream.

Lola turned her over to the doctors and headed straight to the Director's office. She knocked and entered when he acknowledged her.

"Are you sure you can trust her," Lola asked with concern in her voice?

"Time will tell," he replied slowly. "But you must help me. Watch her closely. You have the ability to read her thoughts and you must do so, especially when I am not around."

"Thank you, sir. I'll do what's best."

178

"I know you will, Lola. You're my number one servant now." He noticed a confused look on her face and asked: "What troubles you, my dear?"

"How long did you know that they were sisters?" She asked.

"Since the moment I saw her climb out of that truck from my office window."

"But why did you talk with her? Surely you must have known everything about her, including her operation to———"

"To amuse myself," he said smiling. "It does get boring here you know? From time-to-time I enjoy a refreshing conversation with someone who truly thinks they can outwit me. It's a bit stimulating, keeps me sharp. But come. Let's prepare ourselves. We have some new company coming our way."

Lola stopped at the door with her eyes closed. "Yes, I can see them coming. She doesn't look so good."

179

"I am so pleased that I chose you. You are a special young and lovely assistant. You shall do us a great service."

The Director and Lola left the office and headed for the restaurant, to prepare themselves for the company headed their way. As the bright blue winter moon shone its rays through the dissipating clouds and haunted looking tree limbs, a lone wolf moved cautiously down into the shadows of a fissure not far from the dimly lit building.

And less than ten miles to the north, a teary-eyed woman——battered and bruised from her passed out husband's calloused fists——just passed a sign on the Newport Highway; a sign that read: Spouse Disposal Sight: 7 Miles .

www.ingramcontent.com/pod-product-compliance
Lightning Source LLC
Chambersburg PA
CBHW020847260626
47169CB00003B/1180